"I Need You To Tell Me."

Her voice was no more than a throaty whisper.

"Lord, woman," he said roughly, "does everything have to be difficult with you?"

"Tell me, Logan."

"What, that I want you? That I've thought of you every damn minute of every damn day since you got here?" His voice grew husky and deep. "Do you want me to tell you what those thoughts were, too? They might shock you, Kat. You might turn tail and run."

His words excited her. She stared at him, thankful she'd left the light off. The darkness gave her courage, a boldness she would normally not have felt.

"I won't run."

Dear Reader,

A sexy fire fighter, a crazy cat and a dynamite heroine—that's what you'll find in *Lucy and the Loner*, Elizabeth Bevarly's wonderful MAN OF THE MONTH. It's the next in her installment of THE FAMILY McCORMICK series, and it's also a MAN OF THE MONTH book you'll never forget—warm, humorous and very sexy!

A story from Lass Small is always a delight, and *Chancy's Cowboy* is Lass at her most marvelous. Don't miss out as Chancy decides to take some lessons in love from a handsome hunk of a cowboy!

Eileen Wilks's latest, *The Wrong Wife*, is chock-full with the sizzling tension and compelling reading that you've come to expect from this rising Desire star. And so many of you know and love Barbara McCauley that she needs no introduction, but this month's *The Nanny and the Reluctant Rancher* is sure to both please her current fans...and win her new readers!

Suzannah Davis is another new author that we're excited about, and *Dr. Holt and the Texan* may just be her best book to date! And the month is completed with a delightful romp from Susan Carroll, *Parker and the Gypsy*.

There's something for everyone. So come and relish the romantic variety you've come to expect from Silhouette Desire!

Lucia Macro

Lucia Macro
And the Editors at Silhouette Desire

Please address questions and book requests to:
Silhouette Reader Service
U.S.: 3010 Walden Ave., P.O. Box 1325, Buffalo, NY 14269
Canadian: P.O. Box 609, Fort Erie, Ont. L2A 5X3

BARBARA McCAULEY
THE NANNY AND THE RELUCTANT RANCHER

SILHOUETTE *Desire*

Published by Silhouette Books

America's Publisher of Contemporary Romance

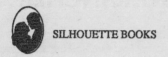

SILHOUETTE BOOKS

ISBN 0-373-76066-3

THE NANNY AND THE RELUCTANT RANCHER

Books by Barbara McCauley

Silhouette Desire

Woman Tamer #621
Man from Cougar Pass #698
Her Kind of Man #771
Whitehorn's Woman #803
A Man Like Cade #832
Nightfire #875
*Texas Heat #917
*Texas Temptation #948
*Texas Pride #971
Midnight Bride #1028
The Nanny and the Reluctant Rancher #1066

*Hearts of Stone

BARBARA McCAULEY

was born and raised in California and has spent a good portion of her life exploring the mountains, beaches and deserts so abundant there. The youngest of five children, she grew up in a small house, and her only chance for a moment alone was to sneak into the backyard with a book and quietly hide away.

With two children of her own now and a busy household, she still finds herself slipping away to enjoy a good novel. A daydreamer and incurable romantic, she says writing has fulfilled her most incredible dream of all: breathing life into the people in her mind and making them real. She has one loud and demanding Amazon parrot named Fred and a German shepherd named Max. When she can manage the time, she loves to sink her hands into fresh-turned soil and make things grow.

For Jennifer Diermendjian.
Thanks, Jen, for all your help and for being who you are.

One

There were three key ingredients to a successful escape: champagne, Oliver and a big hat.

In honor of Katrina Delaney's final performance before her world tour in three months, the first essential element already flowed freely in the spacious New York Marriott Hotel suite. A few extra dollars slipped covertly to the caterer by the guest of honor herself ensured that certain glasses at the elegant party would not be left empty long.

Dressed in a long, black crepe gown—a Larisa Delaney original designed by her mother—Katrina stood on the edge of the buzzing crowd and struggled to tune out the chatter surrounding her. Excitement coursed through her, not because of the party, but because of what would happen when it was over. Her pulse raced and her stomach cartwheeled, but her own glass of bubbly remained untouched. Tonight she needed steady nerves and a clear head. She forced herself to concentrate on the distant sound of Brahms and the scent of roses that filled the suite.

"Katrina, darling, there you are!"

Katrina drew in a fortifying breath at the sound of the familiar voice, then watched Sydney Joyce push her way through a tight circle of people. It wasn't that Katrina didn't like the gossip columnist, in fact, she actually enjoyed the outrageous style of the older woman. But the platinum blond reporter was part bloodhound, and her nose was constantly to the ground, sniffing for a story to delight the fans of celebrity scandal. So far, Sydney had romantically linked the name Katrina Natalya Delaney to Brad Pitt, Richard Gere and Keanu Reeves.

Katrina had met Brad and Richard once at a charity ball, that was it. And as far as Keanu went, they'd merely been at the same party, about as close a relationship as Katrina had had with any man since her one brief, and rather disappointing affair with an English teacher her senior year in college. So much for the exciting social life of a violin virtuoso.

"Katrina, my darling," Sydney purred as she moved in for the kill, "you look absolutely radiant tonight. I refuse to budge until you tell me who the lucky man is."

Katrina sighed. Sydney's words were not a threat, but a promise. If she suspected even the tiniest deception, she'd clamp down like a bulldog and never let go until she got something. Tonight was one night Katrina could not afford to humor the woman.

With the ears of an elephant, Max Straub, Katrina's business manager, quickly moved in. Publicity was the man's job, and every move his clients made, especially Katrina, was carefully orchestrated. Tomorrow, when he found out what she'd done, Katrina knew that Max was not going to be a happy camper.

"What lucky man?" Max looked at Katrina and lowered his dark bushy eyebrows in disapproval.

Katrina hadn't time to respond before her mother and father suddenly joined the growing circle around her. Married in Russia thirty-six years ago, Larisa and Nicolai had immigrated to the States one year before she was born. Katrina had the same amber brown hair as her mother, and though the older Delaney woman was nearly fifty-five, heads still turned when she walked into a room. Katrina's father, darkly handsome and terribly protective of not only his wife, but his only child, as well, scowled constantly at every one of those heads that turned toward wife or daughter.

"A man?" her father asked gruffly. "What's his name?"

"That's what I'm trying to find out." Sydney cut Katrina off before she could speak.

"Don't be ridiculous." Katrina's mother smiled. "Katrina hasn't time right now for that. Do you, dear?"

"Of course, she doesn't," Max answered. "Which reminds me, Katrina, you have a two o'clock tomorrow with Warner Records, a five o'clock with a reporter from the *New York Times* and a six o'clock with a photographer from *Classical Weekly*. I'll pick you up at noon and we'll have lunch to go over the rest of the week's schedule."

Katrina simply nodded, but then, when Max started in on scheduling, there was little to say. He wasn't listening; he was planning.

"I thought you were spending the day with me tomorrow," Katrina's mother said.

"She promised me an interview." Sydney pouted.

"She's practicing tomorrow," her father stated with authority.

They all started to argue then. Katrina sighed, then glanced at the head waiter, who nodded, then promptly refilled everyone's glass standing around her. A hand on her elbow gently tugged her away from the heated discussion surrounding her.

Oliver. *Thank God.* The second essential ingredient had arrived at last.

"You're late," she said quietly.

"Sorry." He kissed her cheek, then brought his lips close to her ear. "That's one hell of a sexy number you've got on, Kat. Sure you don't want to run away and have an adventure with me instead of some bowlegged cowboy?"

Katrina smiled at Oliver's foolishness. They'd met in

high school and gone through college together. He was her best friend, but she knew that his shameless flirting and devilish good looks were going to get the sandy-haired cello player in trouble one day.

"I'm not running away," she whispered. "I'm taking a little vacation by myself, that's all."

Oliver gave a snort of laughter. "Katrina, my love, most people wouldn't call working on a Texas ranch as a nanny to a nine-year-old a vacation."

Katrina watched Max argue with her father over the next day's schedule. "It is to me," she said wistfully.

"You're Katrina Natalya Delaney," Oliver insisted. "Violin virtuoso, the toast of the symphony circuit. A villa in Spain or a town house in France is much more the image."

"I don't give a damn about image." Katrina noticed the conductor of the evening's performance glance over at her. She smiled at him, and he raised his glass to her, then continued his conversation with a music critic from *Entertainment Weekly*.

"Oliver—" she lowered her voice "—I'm twenty-four years old. Music has always been my life. I've never done anything else, been anywhere by myself. In three months I'll be traveling and performing for two years straight, surrounded by people, never a moment to think, let alone be by myself. If I'm going to do this, it has to be now."

"But working on a ranch, Katrina." A waiter carrying a tray of stuffed mushrooms passed by. Oliver reached for one. "Why not a dude ranch or whatever those things are called?" he said when they were alone again. "You could put on some jeans, a cowboy hat and sit on a horse for a couple of days."

"It's not the same," she said emphatically. "Ollie, tell me there isn't something you've wanted to do all your life, something completely different than you've ever done, something wild and crazy and romantic."

He grinned. "Yeah. Swim naked with you in the Thames."

She sighed with exasperation. "I want to experience a real, honest-to-goodness working ranch, with real, honest-to-goodness cowboys, a world completely opposite of my own, where no one will know who I am. The second I saw the ad in that magazine you gave me, and saw that the name of the town was Harmony, it was like a neon sign. I had to apply."

"It's all my fault," Oliver groaned. "I know how crazy you are over that cowboy stuff, and when I saw a copy of *Western Roundup* I thought you'd get a kick out of it. I never dreamed you'd start sending out résumés to be a nanny."

"I could hardly apply for ranch foreman," she said, then waved to Sharon Westphal, a shy flutist who Katrina knew had a crush on Oliver. Katrina had been trying to get Oliver to ask her out, but he'd come up with every excuse he could think of to avoid her. He looked at her now and his eyes took on a strange glint before he quickly turned away and took Katrina's elbow.

"You've never been around kids," Oliver protested, "let alone be a nanny. This guy—what's his name—he'll spot you for a phony in a minute."

"His name is Logan Kincaid, and I'm not a phony. I'm perfectly qualified. You know I minored in English in school and I have a teaching credential. And if that's not enough, I believe that the fact I had three nannies of my own gives me an edge of experience the average nanny wouldn't have."

Oliver laughed. "An average nanny you definitely are not. For that matter, my sweet, there is *nothing* average about you."

She knew he meant it as a compliment, but somehow Oliver's statement disturbed her. She'd hoped that he might understand that was exactly the reason she'd taken this job, because she wanted, if only for a little while, to be like the "average" person. But Oliver had always loved being in the spotlight and performing. It was hard for him to understand that everyone else didn't feel that way. As much as she loved to play, performing in public always made her stomach queasy.

"It's only for two months," she said, feeling the need to defend herself. "I can certainly handle that."

"Oh, sure you can." Oliver reached for a glass of champagne on a passing tray. "And just how do you know this Kincaid guy is not a lecherous old man who'll corral you in the barn and seduce you?"

Katrina laughed. "You should have been a writer instead of a cellist, Ollie. Your imagination is outrageous."

Offended, Oliver lifted his chin. "Are you criticizing my talents as a cellist?"

Poor Oliver. He was as sensitive as he was concerned. "Of course not. You're the best, and you know it, so don't go fishing for compliments. And just to set your active mind at ease, I did have a friend of mine in the police department check out Mr. Kincaid. He's not old, he's thirty-four, he's widowed and he has no criminal record."

"Yet." Oliver frowned. "If your parents or Max find out I know where you are, I'm a dead man."

Katrina slipped an arm through Oliver's and started to lead him toward Sharon. She felt him stiffen immediately. "They don't need to know where I am. I've left letters for them, explaining that it's time I learn to make my own decisions, schedule my own life for a change. Everyone has taken care of me for too long," she said gently, "including you. It might be the coward's way out, but you know there'll be a scene and I'm not going to take any chances I'll weaken. If there's an emergency, you can contact me and I'll call or come home. I'm counting on you, Ollie."

With a sigh of resignation, Oliver slipped an arm around Katrina. "What time is the getaway?"

"Midnight. Everyone will be gone and my parents will be sound asleep in their own room, thanks to all the champagne they've had. We were checking out tomorrow anyway and going home, so my mother didn't think it odd when she noticed I've already packed. I'll be waiting for you outside the front entrance.''

"Someone's going to see you," he said, shaking his head.

"Let me handle that," she whispered in his ear, then steered him toward the flutist. "You just show up on time."

Two hours, twenty-six minutes later, Katrina picked up her suitcases and violin, then crept quietly down the hall and got on the elevator with three other people. She passed at least a dozen more guests in the lobby, then walked by the front desk, the doorman and valet.

Not one person spoke to her or recognized her, but later, the doorman did remember a woman wearing a rather large gray felt hat.

The woman was late.

Swearing under his breath, Logan stood at the large picture window in his living room and stared out at the endless Texas landscape. Heat shimmered off the dry ground and a hawk made lazy circles overhead. Pale gray clouds in the distance suggested rain, but didn't promise. But then, Logan thought with a frown, he'd learned long ago never to trust a promise.

The deep, resonant bong of the grandfather clock in the entry marked eleven o'clock. Logan swore again. The woman should have been here an hour ago.

"She's not coming, is she?"

He turned at the sound of his daughter's soft voice behind him. He never would have shown his impatience if he'd realized she'd been in the room. But it had been after midnight before he'd gotten to bed last night, and he'd been up since five a.m. feeding the livestock and mending fence on the south quarter. He still had a water pump to repair in the west feeding pens, and a missing heifer somewhere in the east section. He was tired as hell and as irritable as a hornet in a jelly jar.

"Of course, she's coming," Logan reassured Anna. Though his daughter rarely complained, he'd sensed her anxiety over meeting Mrs. Lacey's summer replacement. His daughter was a sensitive, quiet child with dove gray eyes that turned his heart to mush every time he looked at her. She'd seen too much disappointment in her young life and he'd die before he'd let anyone hurt her again.

"It's almost a three-hour drive from Dallas to Harmony," he said, moving beside her and tucking one blond curl behind her ear, "then it's another thirty minutes from town to here. Her plane may have come in late, or she may have had to wait to rent a car, but she'll be here, honey, don't worry."

He hated lying to Anna, but he knew he'd only add to her nervousness if he told her that the plane *had* come in on time. He'd called the airlines three hours ago when he'd come in to have breakfast with his daughter, and the plane had arrived not only on time, but ten minutes early. It was certainly possible that she'd changed her mind. Her application had come in over the fax machine in his office, and he'd wondered why a woman from New York City would even consider working on a remote cattle ranch. Normally he wouldn't have even considered her for the job, but he'd only received three responses, and he'd liked hers the best.

Miss Delaney's references from an Oliver Grant had been glowing. Her educational background was more extensive than the other two applicants, though he had to admit he wasn't overly impressed with her degree in music. Still, she also had a degree in English, a course of study certainly appropriate for Anna's education. At fifty-four, she was also older than the other two and able to start right away, while the other women weren't available for several days. Mrs. Lacey had already been gone for two weeks, and while Sophia, the housekeeper, was shopping and helping out with Anna, she was only able to work part-time and was a terrible cook. Anna was barely eating, and he'd lost a few pounds himself. Though cooking had not been in the job description for Anna's nanny, he was hoping a few extra dollars would correct that oversight. If it didn't, he and Anna might starve.

He looked down at his daughter and in spite of his irritation, couldn't help the feeling of tenderness that came over him. If only Anna's mother could have seen her daughter for the wonderful, beautiful little girl she was, perhaps she'd still be here and Anna would have the mother she deserved instead of live-in teachers.

Logan had never understood, nor would he ever understand, how a life on the road, singing in one dive after another, could have been more important to JoAnn than her own daughter. He didn't give a damn for himself that she was gone. The last two years of their marriage had been a living hell, anyway. If anything, he'd been relieved. But to leave Anna, to walk out on her own child, that was something he could never forgive.

"Don't you have some lessons Mrs. Lacey left for you?" he asked his daughter, hoping to distract her.

"I did them already."

"What about the math? I know you were having trouble with division, I can—"

"Daddy, it's summer. Other kids don't have lessons in summer, why do I have to?"

He caught himself before he could say that she wasn't like other kids. She was going to need every advantage that life had to offer, and an education would be her strongest asset. There was nothing he wouldn't do to make sure she had every academic opportunity available to her. He was about to launch into his speech that she'd already heard dozens of times, when the sound of a car horn stopped him.

It was about damn time.

He moved to the window and frowned at the sight of Punch Wilkins's pickup bouncing up the dirt road from the main highway. What the hell was the gas station attendant from Harmony doing here?

Of course. The Delaney woman's rental car must have broken down. He should have considered that. Dust billowed behind Punch's truck as he pulled off the dirt road onto the circular driveway in front of Logan's house. Logan watched Punch hop out of the cab of his truck and reach into the back bed. He pulled out a suitcase and garment bag and another small case. The passenger door of the cab opened, but he couldn't see the woman when she stepped out.

Logan turned to his daughter. "See, honey, I told you—"

But Anna had disappeared. It was no surprise. He knew how difficult it was for her to meet strangers. He'd coax her out later, after he'd spoken to and finalized everything with the new nanny.

He moved to the front door and opened it. Punch stood there, his fist in the air, ready to knock. His large frame blocked Logan's view of the woman standing behind him.

"Howdy," Punch said with a silly grin on his face. "Brought your new nanny to ya."

"Thanks." Logan reached for the suitcase and stepped aside. Punch moved into the entry past Logan and headed for the living room.

A tall, slender, distinctly feminine figure wearing a large gray hat stepped in front of him. *Oh, no,* he groaned silently when he noticed the violin case she held in front of her. *Anything but that.*

Slowly she tipped her head back. When her smoky green eyes met his, his throat went as dry as the dust still swirling outside from Punch's truck.

Who the hell was this woman?

"I'm sorry I'm late," she said with a touch of breath-lessness to her voice. "Transportation here was much more difficult than I'd anticipated. I'm Kat Delaney."

She held out one delicate, finely sculptured hand. In a daze, Logan took it. He had the distinct sensation of silk against sandpaper. Her fingers were long and tapered, her skin smooth and incredibly soft, like nothing he'd ever felt before.

Kat Delaney? This *couldn't* be the woman he'd hired.

She shifted uncomfortably when he said nothing. "You, ah, must be Logan Kincaid."

He had to think for a moment. "There must be some mistake."

She frowned. "You aren't Mr. Kincaid?"

"That's not what I mean." He narrowed his eyes. "I'm talking about you."

"Me?" she said hesitantly, then slipped her hand from his when he didn't let go.

"The woman I hired is supposed to be fifty-four," he said impatiently. "You're not, I mean you aren't—"

"Fifty-four?" She raised one finely arched brow. "I'm *twenty*-four, Mr. Kincaid. That's what I put on the application."

Twenty-four? Logan tried to remember the application. The fax had come in a little fuzzy, but still, how could he have made a mistake like that? He never would have hired a younger woman to take care of Anna. Maturity and experience were a necessary and important element of caring for his daughter. What could a twenty-four-year-old know about raising children?

He stared down at her. She was taller than most women, maybe around five-foot-eight, but still a good eight inches shorter than him. She wore no makeup, but her dark, thick lashes outlined wide, slightly slanted eyes. Her high cheeks glowed with color, though he assumed the heat was responsible for the flush on her skin.

"Hey, Logan," Punch called from the living room, "got a cold one?"

"It's eleven o'clock in the morning, Punch," Logan said with more annoyance than he intended. "There's ice tea in the fridge." He looked at Kat. "Can I, uh, get you something?"

"In a minute, thank you." She swept off her hat. "The ride here with Mr. Wilkins was a bit overwhelming. I just need a minute or two to catch my breath."

So do I, Logan thought as he watched the woman shake her long golden brown curls away from her face. She wore white, the color no more practical on a Texas ranch than her high heels or slim-fitting skirt and tank top. She'd pushed the sleeves of her matching cardigan up to her elbows, revealing long, graceful arms. He would have offered to take her sweater, but since she wasn't staying, he didn't bother.

She might belong on the cover of a fashion magazine, but she sure as hell didn't belong on his ranch.

"Hey, Logan," Punch yelled from the kitchen, "you gonna eat these tamales in here?"

Anyone other than Punch, Logan would have strongly warned against Sophia's cooking. But considering the mood he was in, he needed to vent on someone. "Help yourself," he called back.

He closed the front door, then turned back to the woman standing in front of him, her hat in one hand and a violin case in the other. Damn, but this was awkward.

"Miss Delaney—"

"Kat."

"Kat, I—"

"Hey, Logan, how do you work this here microwave?"

He was going to murder the man. No, better yet, he'd give him the leftover enchiladas to go with the tamales. He looked at Kat and frowned. "I'll be back in a minute."

Kat let loose of the breath she'd been holding when Logan disappeared around the corner. Her insides were shaking and her palms were sweating. She'd given countless performances in front of thousands of people, but never had she been more nervous than she was right now. Her training had taught her to hide her fear, but nothing had ever prepared her for Logan Kincaid.

His height had been the first thing that had taken her aback. He was tall, probably around six-foot-four, with broad shoulders and thickly muscled arms. He wore a denim work shirt, with the sleeves rolled to his elbows, and snug, faded jeans over long, powerfully built legs. His hair was black, his eyes darker than any eyes she'd ever seen. When he'd first looked at her, she'd felt as if she were made of glass, and she might shatter under his piercing gaze.

But the fact that he was handsome wasn't what had

knocked the sense out of her. She met handsome men all
the time. Not one had ever left her weak-kneed or light-
headed. No, Mr. Kincaid was just so...*male*. At the most
basic, the most primitive level, the man exuded virility. He
was a masculine feast for the feminine senses: the rough,
electric texture of his hands, the deep rugged sound of his
voice, the faint, strangely pleasant smell of dust and dirt
and leather. Just looking at him had made her pulse rate
increase, and when he'd held her hand in his, pleasure had
rippled through her entire body.

Had he noticed the color rise to her cheeks? she wondered. Something told her there was very little that Logan
Kincaid missed with those eyes of his. Had Oliver been
right? Could Mr. Kincaid know just by looking at her that
she really wasn't a nanny?

Of course he couldn't. She was just tense. After all, she'd
flown the red-eye, waited three hours for the first bus out
of Dallas to Harmony—which was a four-hour ride—an
hour trying to find someone to drive her here from the
town, and at least thirty minutes bouncing in a truck. She
was also in a completely new environment, meeting a
strange man about a new job.

She had good reason to be high-strung, and that would
certainly explain her physical reaction to Mr. Kincaid, she
told herself. She was just tired and on edge. A good night's
sleep and she'd be fit as a fiddle.

Smiling at her own pun, Kat moved into the living room.
She'd immediately liked the house when Mr. Wilkins had
driven up. It was single story, a redbrick ranch-style struc-
ture with a wide, cement circular driveway and gently slop-
ing gray tile entry. The living room was spacious, with a
high, vaulted ceiling, hardwood floors and a floor-to-ceiling
stone fireplace. The furniture was large and masculine, like
the man himself, and the few pieces of art were a blend of
American Indian and the Old West. It was a warm, comfortable room, *not* like the man himself.

A movement from a doorway across the room caught
Katrina's attention. "Hello?"

There was no answer. With her violin and hat still in her hand, Kat moved toward the doorway. "Hello?" she called again. "Is someone there?"

Again, no answer, but there was a sound, a soft, swooshing sound. Kat stopped, then watched as a young, blond child in a wheelchair appeared in the doorway. She was a beautiful little girl with pale, smooth skin and enormous gray eyes. In her plain brown jumper and white blouse, the child almost blended in with the room.

"Hello." Kat smiled. "I'm Kat."

The child said nothing, just stared at the violin case and hat in Kat's hand.

"What's your name?" Kat moved in front of the little girl and knelt down.

"Anna," she answered quietly.

"Nice to meet you, Anna." Kat put her hand out. Anna stared at it, then slowly put her small hand in Kat's.

"I'm your new nanny," Kat said. "But I'd rather you just thought of me as one of your friends, if that's okay."

"I don't have very many friends," Anna said softly.

Anna's statement didn't surprise Kat. A disabled child living on a ranch outside a small town raised by nannies probably didn't get to meet a lot of other children. Neither did a child prodigy living in New York with well-meaning, but ambitious parents.

"I don't have very many friends, either," Kat said warmly. "But we each have one new one, starting right now."

Anna smiled shyly. "You don't look like a nanny."

Kat laughed. "Thanks, I think."

"Is that a violin?" Anna stared at the case in Kat's hand.

"Why, yes it is, would you like to—"

"Miss Delaney."

Kat jumped up at the sound of Logan's voice behind her. She had no idea why he would be, but she could have sworn he sounded angry.

Logan's tight expression softened when he looked at his daughter. "Anna, I've asked Sophia to make you some lunch. Why don't you go on in the kitchen and say hello to Punch while I speak with Miss Delaney.''

Anna looked from her father to Kat, then nodded reluctantly and left the room. When Logan turned to her and frowned, Kat felt a tremor of apprehension low in her stomach.

"You have a beautiful daughter, Mr. Kincaid.''

"Thanks.'' Logan sighed and ran a hand through his hair. "Look, Miss Delaney—''

He'd called her by her formal name three times in the past two minutes. Something was wrong, she realized. Very wrong.

"—I know you came a great distance to get here. It's not an easy drive to Harmony, and riding with Punch was no picnic, either, I'm sure.''

Something told her he wasn't about to discuss the discomfort of her transportation here. She drew in a slow, deep breath to steady herself, certain she wasn't going to like whatever it was he was going to say. "Why don't you just get to the point, Mr. Kincaid.''

"I'm afraid you aren't going to work out, after all.''

Her heart sank. He knew. That had to be it. He knew she'd never been a nanny, maybe even figured out somehow what she really did do, and that while she hadn't lied on her application about anything, she had withheld information about herself that he might consider important.

She struggled to keep her voice even and her shoulders straight. "And may I ask why?''

"It's my fault completely,'' Logan said with obvious difficulty. "There were some streaks in the fax transmission you sent, and I misread the application. I thought you were older.''

He was letting her go because she was too young, not because he knew who she was? Relief washed through her, then disbelief.

"Let me get this straight,'' she said, struggling to keep her voice even. "I fly hundreds of miles, wait three hours for a bus that I ride on for almost four hours, then hire

Wildman Wilkins to drive me here, and you're telling me you've changed your mind because I'm too young?''

"Look, Miss Delaney, I'm sorry about this. I'll pay for any expenses you've incurred, and give you a week's salary. That should take care of any inconvenience I've caused you.''

She couldn't believe this. After all she'd gone through to get here, everything she'd planned, he was firing her? "You're *sorry?*'' she repeated. "A *week's* salary?''

His eyes narrowed. "All right, then, two weeks'.''

She had to choke back the hysterical laughter bubbling in her throat. "Are you saying you'd rather pay me off, than give me a chance?''

"I've admitted I made a mistake,'' he said stiffly. "Anna needs someone older, with more experience.''

Of all the stubborn— Katrina took a calming breath and leveled her gaze with his. "Was there anything else you *misread* on my application or credentials? Something that you find objection to?''

He hesitated. "No.''

"Do you have someone else for this job?''

A muscle jumped in his jaw. "Not at the moment.''

"Then who's going to take care of Anna until you find someone?''

Logan had already been asking himself that very question. He did need someone. Now, not next week or the week after. But he had no intention of hiring someone as young as Kat Delaney, and certainly not someone as pretty.

He surprised himself by that thought. It wasn't as if he didn't know that he could control his baser instincts...he could. But he'd been busy with the ranch and Anna, and he'd been without female companionship for a long time. A woman who looked like Kat might be a distraction. A distraction he didn't want, and he sure as hell didn't need.

He could hardly tell her that, though. *Gee, Miss Delaney, I can't hire you because I'd like to drag you to my bed.*

"I have a part-time housekeeper. We'll manage until I find someone else.'' They might starve to death, he thought, but somehow he would manage. "I'll have Punch drive you back to town," he said evenly. "I can give you a check now or send it to the address on your application."

Her green eyes darkened as she lifted her chin. "Don't bother. I don't want your money, and I have no intention of going home. I came here to Harmony to work for the summer and that's what I intend to do. I'm sure I'll find something else."

Logan shook his head. "You can't be serious. Harmony is a small town. There won't be much use for a violin-toting nanny."

"I'm a hard worker, Mr. Kincaid. Reliable and trust-worthy. Qualities that most people admire."

Logan frowned. She'd emphasized the word trustworthy, the implication being that he wasn't. She was wrong for the job, dammit. That didn't make him dishonest or un-scrupulous. "Maybe I should drive you back to town. I could—"

"No, thank you." She jammed her hat on her head and struggled to pick up both of her suitcases. "Please tell Mr. Wilkins I'll wait for him in the truck. Good day to you."

He would have offered to carry her luggage for her, but something told him if he tried, he just might have a violin crammed down his throat.

She stopped at the door, and without turning around, said quietly, "Would you object to my visiting Anna while I'm in Harmony? Maybe just for an occasional afternoon, or sometime when you come into town?"

Her question caught him off guard, then settled over him like a net of guilt. "You can come here anytime you want."

She nodded, then wrestled with her suitcases while she opened the front door and closed it behind her. Logan started after her, then stopped and swore heatedly. He'd already admitted to her he'd made a mistake, he had no intention of going after the woman and trying to explain further.

Why the hell should he feel guilty? He'd offered com-pensation, hadn't he? And he certainly didn't believe she would actually stay in Harmony. She was a city girl. One day in a sleepy little town like Harmony and the woman would be on her way.

Whatever she did, it didn't matter to him. He had no time to think about a curvy, green-eyed brunette with incredible legs. There were more important things to worry about right now, such as finding an appropriate nanny for Anna.

With a heavy sigh, Logan went to the kitchen to get Punch, wondering where in the hell he was going to find the perfect woman.

Two

She wasn't going home.

Suitcases at her feet, Kat sat on a wooden bench in front of the Harmony Hay and Feed and Hardware Store. A few of the townspeople had passed by and given her odd looks, several had even asked if she needed help. She'd wanted to tell them it wasn't she who needed help, it was a pigheaded rancher named Logan Kincaid.

Damn the man! He needed someone for Anna, that was obvious. With a ranch and house his size, how could he possibly manage? A part-time housekeeper wasn't enough, he wouldn't have advertised for a nanny if it were.

If she hadn't met Anna, Kat might not have taken Logan's rejection so hard. But in the few minutes she'd spoken with the child, Kat had felt a connection she couldn't explain, and wasn't sure she understood. It was something in Anna's soft gray eyes, a need, or a loneliness. Maybe Kat even saw herself. Whatever it was, she'd nearly cried when Logan had told her he didn't want her.

But she hadn't cried, and even if Mr. Logan Kincaid had

drastically altered her plans, she was determined to go through with her stay in Harmony. Everything was just as she'd imagined it. Wide, open spaces, deep blue sky. The people were friendly and no one seemed to be in much of a hurry—except Punch Wilkins. The man drove like a New York City cabdriver. Her fingers were still clenched from holding on to the truck door.

In spite of Logan Kincaid, Kat was glad she'd come here. So it was impetuous, and maybe even a little reckless. For once in her life, just once, she wanted to be unpredictable, have a little excitement. No schedules, no meetings, no practices. No one had a piece of her here. She answered only to herself, made her own choices, good or bad.

She wouldn't go home! She *couldn't!* How could she face her parents, or Max or Oliver, if she gave up now? She had to take charge of her own life, make her own decisions, even if they were bad ones.

Sighing, Kat sat back on the hard wooden bench and looked around. Punch had dropped her off here, next to the bus depot because Logan had told him to. Obviously the man hadn't believed she really would stay. But he was wrong. She could be just as stubborn as he was. She noticed a small motel at the end of the street, the Harmony Motel. Right next door was the Harmony Café. A large sign in the window of the café caught her attention: Waitress Wanted.

Smiling, Kat picked up her bags and crossed the street.

Anna wouldn't eat. She hadn't said a word in two days, and for that matter, she hadn't even looked at him. She'd stayed in her room, even refusing his offer to take her with him to town today for ice cream. Logan had been tempted to make her come with him; he knew she wouldn't have argued if he'd insisted. But he hadn't wanted to force her, so he'd driven into Harmony for a load of grain by himself, trying his damnedest to think of a way to cheer his daughter up, other than to give her what he knew she really wanted, which was Kat Delaney.

He'd been surprised when he'd seen Anna talking to the

woman two days ago. Anna rarely spoke to people she didn't know, and for that matter, hardly spoke to people she did know. He'd seen the disappointment in her eyes when he'd told her that Miss Delaney wouldn't be staying. When Anna had asked if it was something she'd said that had made Miss Delaney leave, or if the woman hadn't liked her, Logan had spent the next hour trying to explain that of course it wasn't anything she'd said, and of course Miss Delaney liked her. He'd then tried to explain, though awkwardly, that he'd decided the woman just wasn't the right nanny, right for her. He'd told her that he called another nanny and she'd be coming in a few days, but from that moment on, Anna had retreated to her room, and she'd only picked at the food he'd insisted she eat.

He flipped on the truck radio to a country and western station, then tipped his hat back with a sigh. As hard as it was to admit it, he felt like a heel sending the Delaney woman away, in spite of her being too young. He'd seen the disappointment in her eyes and her forced attempt at bravado when he'd fired her. She'd come a long way, and she'd certainly seemed eager. He could have kept her on, at least given her a chance. But his initial response to her had been so strong he hadn't thought logically. His firing her had been more like a knee-jerk reaction than a rational decision.

No, he'd made the right decision, dammit. He was only human, for God's sake. A woman who looked like Kat Delaney under his roof would be too big a distraction. Since he could hardly explain that to Anna, she was just going to have to accept his decision.

Logan swung off the main road and headed into town. It was ridiculous, but as he drove past the bus depot he found himself looking for a slender brunette with a big gray hat, as if she'd still be sitting on the bench there. He shook his head at his foolishness. She might have told him that she'd be staying in Harmony, but he hadn't believed her. Once she realized there were no jobs for her, and she didn't fit in here, that bus ride back to the Dallas airport would be looking mighty good. He figured she'd come to that decision about fifteen minutes after Punch had dropped her off.

He forced the woman from his mind and turned his thoughts back to his daughter. As soon as he loaded the truck, he'd make a trip over to Johnson's Department Store and pick something out for her, maybe a new game for her computer, or that jewelry-making kit she had her eye on last trip into town. Hell, he'd buy them both. He'd do anything to bring a smile to her face.

As he pulled into town, Logan passed Marge Baker, Harmony's librarian, and waved at her. She stopped in the middle of her sweeping, put a fist on her ample hip and frowned at him.

"What's her problem?" Logan wondered aloud, but knowing how crabby the woman was anyway, paid no attention. He had some books at the house, maybe they were overdue. He'd better check when he got home, or she might send the sheriff after him.

At the hay and feed, though, Mike Carson hardly said a word to him, and his son, Jessie, had ignored him when he'd helped load the truck. Maybe it was just his own bad mood reflecting off everyone else, he decided.

The smell of hamburgers drifted to him from the café across the street and his stomach growled in response. After Sophia's cooking, one of Stubbs Parson's big juicy burgers was like a gourmet meal. He'd grab a little lunch for himself, order something for Anna, then make a quick stop at the department store before heading home. Between the food and presents, he'd have his daughter smiling before the sun went down.

The bell tinkled overhead as Logan entered the café. The lunch crowd had filled most of the tables, but Logan found a spot at the counter and slid onto a stool. He turned the coffee cup already sitting in front of him right side up, then picked up a menu and studied it, trying to figure out what Anna would like.

Coffee magically appeared in his cup, and a soft, silky voice asked, "What can I get for you, Mr. Kincaid?"

Logan went still, then slowly lowered the menu and stared into eyes the color of spring sage.

Well, I'll be damned.

Kat Delaney.

She wore a blue waitress uniform, much shorter than he thought appropriate, though he never recalled having that thought with Ellen, the usual waitress. But, of course, he'd never interviewed Ellen to be Anna's nanny, either.

He couldn't believe she was still here.

She'd pulled her hair back into a ponytail, emphasizing her large green eyes and thick lashes. The color rising on her cheeks matched the pink of her lips. He had to make a conscious effort not to stare at those lips.

He tipped his hat to her and forced his voice to be even. "Miss Delaney."

"Oh, you can call me Kat," she said cheerfully, pointing to her name tag. "Everyone else here does."

His eyes went to the name tag pinned neatly to her snug-fitting uniform, directly over her full breasts. He ground his back teeth together.

"Hey, Katie, darlin', my cup's empty," Rusty Burke called from a booth. "How 'bout a refill?"

"Be right back." She grinned at Logan and with her coffeepot in hand, sauntered over to the obnoxious man.

He watched her smile at Rusty and felt the heat rise under his collar. What the hell was a woman like her doing here, talking to guys like that? Was she too damn innocent to know what men like Rusty wanted? It sure wasn't a cup of coffee.

His hand closed tightly around his own coffee cup. Who knew better than him? he thought angrily. He'd certainly wanted a hell of a lot more than coffee himself. But at least he knew he wouldn't do anything about it. The same was not true of Rusty, or a dozen other local cowboys. She had no idea what she was getting herself into, waiting on these men and smiling at them the way she was.

She came back and pulled a pencil and pad from her pocket. "What can I get for you?"

Logan nearly groaned. If she asked that question all day long to this group, she was in for trouble.

"Hey, Katie," another man called from a table. "You got any honey?"

Logan turned on the man and growled. "Get it yourself. She's helping me."

Kat raised one eyebrow, but said nothing, waiting with her pencil poised.

"I'll have a hamburger," he said sourly.

"Would you like it cooked?" she asked sweetly, "or shall I just toss it through the bars?"

He frowned at her, but when she turned away, he reached across the counter for her arm and gently pulled her back. She was right, he was being surly. She didn't deserve it now any more than she'd deserved being fired two days ago.

"I wasn't expecting to see you here." He wished they were anywhere but the middle of a crowded café.

She smiled slowly, and the soft upward curve of her lips made his pulse jump. "I admit, I'm a little surprised myself. If it wasn't for Mr. Parson, I might have given up. He's been wonderful to me."

And I haven't, Logan thought with a frown. Her skin was soft and smooth where he held her arm. He knew he should let go, but he couldn't seem to break the contact between them.

"Look, Miss Delaney—Kat," he said as quietly as he could over the clatter of dishes and people talking. "About the other day. I didn't mean to be rude or unreasonable. I just…well, you weren't what I was expecting."

She looked at him for a long moment, then sighed softly and relaxed her shoulders. "How's Anna?"

"Logan Kincaid, get your hands off my waitress!"

Stubbs Parson came around from behind the grill waving a spatula, his bulldog face scowling.

"Don't think you can come in here and steal this gem

away from me, especially after the way you've treated her, Mr. Flimflam man. Word has it from Punch Wilkins you brought her all the way from New York, then fired her faster than he could microwave a tamale.''

Logan and Stubbs had been friends for years, and Logan, like everyone else in town, had always tolerated and been amused by the ornery old café owner. At the moment, however, Logan definitely didn't feel very tolerant, and he sure as hell didn't feel amused. He ignored Stubbs and looked directly at Kat. Her face was bright red and it was obvious that everyone in town knew he'd fired her. No wonder people had been treating him like a pariah. With that innocent face of hers, and that sweet smile, Logan Kincaid would look like the devil incarnate. Logan decided he was going to strangle Punch.

He also decided he wanted Kat Delaney back.

For Anna, of course.

"How much is he paying you?" Logan asked Kat.

Flustered, Kat looked at Stubbs. "Well, I—"

"Oh, no, you don't." Stubbs waved his spatula at Logan. "To quote Punch, you said that you needed someone older. Well, mister, she might be too young for you, but she's not for me."

"I'm not too young for you, sweetie," Stella Jones, the town beautician said from the booth behind him. Stella had to be at least sixty, with brassy red hair and a cosmetics-counter face. Logan's collar was burning now, and the heat moved like wildfire up his neck. He decided he wasn't going to strangle Punch. That would be too quick. He was going to kill him slowly and painfully.

"How much is he paying you?" Logan asked Kat again.

"The tips have been very generous," Kat said carefully.

"I'll bet they have." Logan looked around the café and saw several of the men staring at Kat. She was probably making twice what he'd offered her.

Crow was a hard dish to swallow, but for Anna, he'd swallow the whole damn bird, beak and all. His daughter wanted Kat, and he'd bring her back come hell or high water.

He held Kat's gaze. "Name your price."

Kat started to open her mouth, but Stubbs cut her off with a wave of his spatula. "Man's gotta pay for his own stupidity, Katie. You wanna go with him, it's okay, but you let me handle this."

Kat was too stunned to say a word when Stubbs handed her a coffeepot and told her to go refill some cups. She wanted to protest, but he was her boss, after all. At least, she *thought* he was. She watched Logan and Stubbs arguing, but they'd lowered their voices and she couldn't hear what they were saying. She knew Logan was angry from the twitch in his temple and the tight set of his jaw. Stubbs, on the other hand, seemed to be having a good time giving Logan a bad time.

The café owner had been good to her these past two days. After she'd checked into the motel next door, she'd applied for the job as waitress. She'd told Stubbs that she'd had no experience, but he hadn't cared and had hired her on the spot. He was a gruff old man with a rough face and a kind heart. He'd slapped the hands of every cowboy and male customer who'd teased her or made even the slightest sexual innuendo. In spite of their flirtations, the cowboys had been gentlemen, and the locals had all been very accepting of a gal from New York City. Everyone was friendly and warm and liked to talk, something New Yorkers hadn't the time for.

And while working in a restaurant hadn't exactly been her dream of coming west and working on a ranch, it had still been interesting to experience a different type of job, one that she'd never really considered. It was a hard, on-your-feet-never-stop job that required physical strength, tremendous patience and a good memory. From now on, she'd definitely have nothing but the utmost regard for all restaurant workers.

But in spite of the fact that she'd enjoyed her two days at the café, she missed Anna. She'd been planning on a visit her next day off, but transportation was still a problem. The thought of riding with Punch made her teeth ache, but to see Anna, she'd tolerate even Wildman's driving.

And now Logan was here. Her knees had started shaking when she'd watched him walk into the diner. The look on his face when he'd seen her had been priceless, but the look he'd given her a moment later, a look that consumed her, had turned her shaking knees to water. She was scared she was going to beg him to hire her again, then suddenly he was actually asking her to come back. She would have said yes in a second. She didn't want more money, she would pay him to let her come back and be with Anna, but out of loyalty to Stubbs and the kindness he'd shown her, she was willing to go along with whatever game he was playing.

Logan's voice grew louder and several heads turned in his direction. He scowled at everyone, then tossed a couple of bills down and stormed out of the café.

Kat's heart sank. He'd changed his mind again. She felt moisture burning in her eyes, but quickly blinked it back. Two rejections in three days from the man was almost enough to have her packing her bags. But she wouldn't. Not because of Mr. Logan Kincaid.

Stubbs picked up the money Logan had thrown down and walked over to where she was clearing a booth. Shaking his head, he looked at her and sighed. "Sorry, Katie. I was shooting for double pay, and only got you half again as much."

It took a moment for his words to sink in. Her heart started pounding. "You mean, he, that I—"

He grinned. "Yep. Looks like you're working for Logan again. We're gonna miss you here, honey, but you and I both know that's not why you came to Harmony, and you don't belong in here waiting tables."

Kat couldn't believe it. She was really going back to the ranch, to Anna. Her head was spinning. "I'll just finish up here today and—"

"'Fraid not. He's waiting outside, and unless I want

that crazy man coming back in here and bothering my customers again, you better hightail it out of here.'' He tucked
the bills Logan had thrown down on the counter into her
pocket. "Here's your tip, darlin'. If he so much as looks
cross-eyed at you, you got a job here anytime.''

"Hey, how 'bout some coffee here, Katie?'' a man
yelled from a booth.

Kat started for the coffeepot, but Stubbs stopped her and
yelled back at the man. "Hold yer horses, McDermott. Katie doesn't work here anymore. You're gonna have to put
up with my mug for a while.''

A chorus of groans shot through the café. Kat laughed
and hugged Stubbs. "I don't know how to thank you.
You're a true gentleman.''

"Dang,'' he said with a lopsided grin, "I been called a
lot things, but never a gentleman.''

"You're gonna be called a lot more things if you don't
get me my food,'' a ranch hand called out.

"Go somewhere else if you don't like the service,''
Stubbs hollered. Since there was nowhere else in town to
go for lunch, the man tucked his hat low on his head and
hunkered down in his seat, grumbling under his breath.

Kat's hands were shaking as she moved behind the
counter and untied her apron. "I'll bring your uniform back
before I leave.''

Stubbs shrugged. "Next time you come into town is fine.
The way Logan is champing at the bit, you better just get
packed. Oh, by the way, Katie, there's one thing Logan
wanted he wouldn't budge on. Since he's paying you more,
it didn't seem too unreasonable.''

"What's that?'' She tossed her apron on a hook under
the counter.

"He wants you to cook.''

"Cook?'' She swallowed hard. "You mean, as in prepare the meals?''

Stubbs ignored Rusty, who was lifting up his coffee cup
for a refill. "You don't like to cook?''

"Of course I like to cook," she said quickly. "I love to cook. I, ah, just don't know what to make, that's all."

"The usual. Meat and potatoes, same thing most men like," he said offhandedly, then cleared his throat and lowered his voice. "You come back and visit us, you hear?"

Kat kissed Stubbs on both cheeks. He turned bright red, then turned and scowled at the round of catcalls that went through the café.

She grabbed her purse and forced herself to walk slowly and calmly out the front door when she really felt like running. Logan turned when she came out, and his expression was tight. No doubt he hated admitting he'd been wrong, and even more, hated asking her to come back at a higher salary. She didn't want the raise, of course, and if he hadn't looked as if he'd bite her head off, she might have told him so. She'd tell him later, when his pride wasn't so sore.

"I'll just be a few minutes," she told him. "I need to pack."

He nodded. "I'm going to the department store. I'll be back in fifteen minutes."

Fifteen minutes? She couldn't pack that fast. "Fine."

He was back in fourteen minutes and she was waiting in front of the motel, wondering what was taking him so long.

They were quiet on the ride back to the ranch. Eyes glued straight ahead, Logan held the steering wheel as if it might come off, and Kat kept her attention on the passing scenery, struggling to control her excitement that he was actually bringing her back. Cows and horses grazed along the barbed-wire fence separating the highway from the land, and wisps of white clouds streaked the blue sky. The weather was pleasantly warm, and Logan drove with his window down. A breeze whipped at Kat's hair, and in spite of her nervousness, she felt a sense of exhilaration. She knew it was silly, but she almost felt as if she were coming home.

"I'll reimburse you for your stay in town," Logan said unexpectedly, breaking the silence after several minutes.

She glanced sideways at him, but he kept his eyes on the road. "That's not necessary."

"If I ever want to check out another library book, buy a hamburger for myself or grain for my stock, it *is* necessary. The entire town thinks I'm some kind of a blackguard, lower than a tick on a dog's—" he stopped himself "—behind."

Startled, Kat turned to look at him. "Because of me?"

He turned off the main highway, onto the road that led to his ranch. "I never expected you to stay in Harmony. When you did, I suddenly became Simon Legree, throwing a damsel in distress into the street."

"Is that why you rehired me?" Kat hated how small her voice sounded. "Because of the town?"

"No." He pulled up in front of the house and cut the engine. "We'll tell Anna you're here, then I'll get you settled in your room."

In her hurry to leave town, Kat hadn't changed out of her uniform, and only now, as Logan opened the cab door for her, did she realize how short her skirt was. She pulled it down, but not before she saw Logan's frown as his gaze moved over her legs. When he offered his hand, she quickly slid out of the truck.

"I didn't have time to change," she said weakly, tugging on the skirt.

He simply shrugged and moved around to get her luggage from the bed of the truck. *Terrific,* she thought with a silent groan. If it wasn't enough she'd made a bad first impression by being younger than he'd expected, her second impression as a floozy wasn't looking so good, either.

"Hey, Logan! You get lost?"

Kat turned as a man approached the truck. He was almost as tall as Logan and about the same age, with dark features and long black hair pulled into a ponytail at the base of his neck. He moved beside the truck and stared at her curiously.

"This is my foreman, Tom Whitefeather," Logan said

as he pulled her luggage out of the truck. "Tom, this is Kat Delaney, Anna's nanny for the summer."

Tom seemed momentarily surprised, then smiled at her and touched the brim of his white cowboy hat. "How do, ma'am."

Kat offered her hand to Tom. "A pleasure to meet you, Mr. Whitefeather."

Tom hesitated, then slowly covered her small hand with his large one. "Just Tom will do, Miss Delaney."

She smiled. "And I'm Kat."

"You think we might move this along anytime soon?" Logan drawled, his arms loaded with Kat's luggage.

"You need some help with that, boss?"

"I think I can manage," he said sarcastically, then turned and headed for the house. "But the truck needs unloading. I'll meet you in the barn in a few minutes."

Tom nodded to her, then hopped in the truck and drove off. Kat threw her hat on her head and hurried after Logan.

The scent of floor cleaner and furniture polish filled the house, along with the sound of a woman singing in Spanish. Logan disappeared through the doorway where Anna had first appeared, and Kat followed. Still holding her luggage, Logan nodded to the end door, which was ajar. The woman's voice was coming from that room.

Nervous, but excited, Kat knocked lightly on the door.

"Come in, Señor Logan," Logan's housekeeper called. "I make *la señorita* Anna *muy bonita.*"

Kat opened the door and entered. Sophia, an older, heavy-boned woman with short, salt-and-pepper hair, stood with her back to the door, combing Anna's hair into a ponytail. Anna sat in her wheelchair beside her pink-and-white canopy bed.

"Anna," Logan said from behind Kat, "I've brought someone with me I thought you might like to say hello to."

With an obvious lack of real interest, Anna turned. When her gaze fell on Kat, the child's eyes lighted. She looked quickly at her father, her expression hopeful, but questioning.

"Miss Delaney is going to stay for the summer," Logan said, his voice softening.

Anna looked at Kat again and smiled slowly. Kat smiled back. "Anna and I are friends, she can call me Kat. And you must be Sophia." Kat looked at the housekeeper.

Sophia nodded, holding onto the ponytail she was assembling. "Welcome to *la casa* Kincaid."

Kat nodded. "Thank you."

"Anna—" Logan smiled at his daughter and Kat realized it was the first time she'd actually seen him do anything but frown "—I'm going to show Miss Delaney her room right now. She'll be back as soon as she gets settled."

Anna nodded, and the ponytail Sophia held fell apart. Anna looked contrite, but Sophia simply shook her head and started over.

Kat followed Logan to the opposite end of the hall. Her bedroom was large and sunny, the hardwood floor polished to a soft shine. Navajo print rugs lay beside, and at the foot of, the king-size bed. She nearly gasped as she looked out the French door slider and saw a private patio with a built-in spa.

Kat had been surrounded her entire life with swank and elegance, and while she'd lived in upscale New York apartments her entire life, none of the rooms had ever been this big, let alone the bedroom. She moved closer to the French doors and stared out onto the patio. And a spa!

She turned to Logan who was hanging her garment bag in the closet. "Good heavens," she said a little breathlessly, "if this is the servant's quarters, I can't wait to see your bedroom."

The second the words were out, Kat wanted them back. He glanced at her, and she could have sworn the corner of his mouth twitched. She felt the rush of heat over her cheeks. "I mean, everything here's just so big...just like they say..." Her voice trailed off.

"Mrs. Lacey, Anna's regular nanny, has the guest room on the other side of the house. Rather than disturb her things, I put you in here." The humor left his eyes. "This used to be my bedroom. I moved out after my wife was killed."

"I'm sorry," Kat said quietly. "It must be very painful for you and Anna."

He moved to the French doors and opened them, then stood there and stared out onto the patio. "My wife left Anna and me long before she died. Anna barely remembers her, and as far as I go, I don't much give a damn."

His voice was cold and empty and when he turned, there was no expression on his face. "I put the spa in for Anna, it helps to exercise her legs. Feel free to use it anytime you like, also. I'll show you how to run it later."

He stood there for a moment, his gaze skimming over her. She'd been on display enough years to understand and accept that look. With any other man she would have casually accepted the male approval she saw in his eyes and shrugged it off.

But he wasn't any other man, and she faltered under the heat of his stare. Her breathing felt shallow and her pulse quickened. The waitress uniform she wore suddenly felt not only too short, but too tight. Her *skin* felt too tight. And when he brought his dark gaze back to hers, her heart skipped a beat.

He shook his head and frowned. "You don't look like a nanny."

Anna had said the same thing to her, she realized. But there was no softness to Logan's words and she realized he wasn't giving her a compliment. "I'll do a good job."

He nodded, then moved toward the door. "I'll get back in around six. I'd like dinner ready by six-thirty."

"Mr. Kincaid?"

He stopped and turned to look at her. A smile touched one corner of his mouth. "Why don't you just call me Logan? Everyone else here does."

She couldn't help but smile, too, as she remembered that was what she'd said to him in the cafe. He started to leave again when she stopped him again.

"Logan," she said quietly, "you never answered my

question earlier. Why did you change your mind and bring me back here?"

He held her gaze, then said, "Anna wasn't happy."

For a moment, she almost thought he was going to say something else. Instead he turned and walked out the door.

Kat let loose of the breath she'd been holding. He didn't want her here. He'd certainly made that clear. With a heavy sigh, she opened her suitcase and started to unpack.

It didn't matter, she told herself. She wasn't here for Logan Kincaid, she was here for Anna, and to experience life from a different perspective, to try new things.

And speaking of new things...she glanced at her watch. She had approximately four hours to learn how to cook.

Three

Logan came in at five that afternoon. He was dirty, tired and more than a little tense. He and three of his men had moved half of the herd to another pasture, and one stubborn steer had broken away, leading Logan on a merry chase through a steep gully and heavy brush. He'd used every epithet in his rather extensive cow cutter's vocabulary twice before he finally escorted the wayward animal back to its bellowing companions, but the fun and games had cost his gelding a shoe and forced Logan to ride back early.

Closing the stall door behind him, he tossed his horse a fleck of hay, then made his way to the house.

It was hard to admit, but Logan knew he was the only one to blame for his troubles. It had been his lack of focus on his work, not a runaway steer that had caused his problems. His mind had been on a curvy green-eyed gal from New York, a woman with long sleek legs that were made for a man to wrap around his waist. When he'd caught sight of those legs earlier as he'd helped her out of the truck, it had taken every ounce of willpower not to openly stare.

He'd wanted to take her back to town right then and there. He'd wanted to take her to bed.

But he'd done neither, of course. And he wouldn't. He would endure a little masculine torture if it made Anna happy. The smile on his daughter's face this afternoon when she'd seen Kat had made every uncomfortable moment worthwhile. He was determined to make it through the summer, even if it cost him a few sleepless nights and several cold showers.

He still couldn't believe she'd stayed in Harmony. Obviously Kat Delaney was a determined woman. While he didn't understand it, he couldn't help but admire her tenacity. He hadn't taken her seriously, and his reputation with the town was smarting from his mistake. *Mistakes,* he corrected himself. His first one had been bringing her here in the first place.

He caught the delicious scent of roast beef and heard laughter when he came in the service entrance off the kitchen. Normally, after a day's work, he would clean up and take off his boots before he went to his room to shower. Today, he stopped, listening to the cheerful sounds coming from the kitchen. Quietly he went to the door and opened it a crack.

He saw Anna first, her face and arms covered with flour, sitting at the kitchen table in a regular chair instead of her wheelchair. Bottom lip between her teeth, she methodically worked a large ball of dough. Bowls and measuring cups surrounded her, as did shortening, salt and an assortment of other baking supplies. It looked as if a bag of flour had exploded.

"Knead about ten times—" Logan heard Kat say "—biscuit dough should feel light and soft, but not sticky..."

Logan turned his attention to Kat and his stomach went into a skid. Dressed in snug-fitting jeans and a white T-shirt, she stood at the kitchen sink, reading from a cookbook while she peeled potatoes. The strings of an apron lay in a neat bow on her flour-dusted backside. His throat felt as dry as the flour as he stared at her well-rounded derriere and long legs encased in tight denim.

"Seven...eight..." he heard his daughter slowly counting as she kneaded the dough.

They were cooking together, he realized in amazement. To the best of his knowledge, Anna had never done anything more in the kitchen than help Sophia set the table. And here she was with Kat—making biscuits?

A feeling he couldn't identify tightened Logan's chest as he watched Anna and Kat. There was a brightness in Anna's eyes, a pinkness in her cheeks that he hadn't seen in a long time. It had never dawned on him that helping in the kitchen might be something she would enjoy. Obviously it had never dawned on anyone else, either. He made a mental note to discuss it with Mrs. Lacey when she came back.

"Is this good?" Anna asked.

Still unobserved, Logan watched Kat set down the potato she'd been peeling, wipe her hands on her apron, then pick up the cookbook and walk over to Anna.

Kat poked at the dough. "You tell me. You're the expert biscuit maker."

"But I've never cooked anything before," Anna said, her brow furrowed.

"Me, either." Kat blew a long strand of hair from her forehead, then reached for a rolling pin on the table and handed it to Anna. "That's how we learn new things. We just do it. Now roll."

Kat had never cooked before? Confused, Logan watched as she read to Anna and the two of them discussed the recipe instructions. She *didn't* know how to cook, he realized. But then, why did she agree to cook for him? Of course, now that he thought about it, he'd never given her a chance to say no. He'd assumed she knew how. After all, even people in New York had to eat.

But then, hadn't he learned by now that any assumption regarding a woman was bound to get a man into trouble?

So she didn't know how to cook. She was here to teach

Anna, that was most important. As long as the woman focused on educating his daughter, he'd put up with indigestion for a few weeks.

And cold showers, he thought when Kat set the cookbook down and rubbed her fists against the small of her back. He had to force back a groan as her full breasts pressed tightly against her T-shirt.

It was going to be a long, painful summer.

With a sigh, he quietly backed away before Anna or Kat spotted him. As he closed the door behind him, he heard them singing, "Roll, roll, roll your dough..."

Kat held her breath as Logan took a bite of the roast she'd cooked. She knew it was silly, that it should matter so much. She'd been to dinners with politicians and celebrities and even royalty, but no dinner had ever made her so nervous, or been so important, as this one. Her first roast, she thought with excitement, watching him chew. And chew.

And chew.

Disappointed, she sank back in her chair. She'd been praying he liked his meat well-done, as in *very* well-done. Rather than torture the man, she should have just told him the truth about her culinary skills. She could see the headlines now: Katrina Delaney, World-Famous Violinist, Poisons Texas Rancher.

"Logan—" she sat straight and stared at her own plate "—I should have—"

"How 'bout another slice of meat?" He popped a bite of beef in his mouth, then scooped up some mashed potatoes and gravy that Kat knew had more lumps than a sugar bowl.

She waited for him to choke, then watched as he simply scooped up another big bite.

Stunned, she handed him the meat platter. He speared a piece of meat, then waved his fork at the bread basket. "And a couple more biscuits, too, please. It's odd,

Grandma Betty used to make biscuits as flaky as these, but she said only the women in my family had the knack.''

Anna, who had been sitting on the edge of her seat also, looked at Kat and smiled.

"Anna made them," Kat said, grinning back at Anna.

Kat could have sworn she saw the devil dance in Logan's eyes as he raised his eyebrows with surprise.

"No." He picked up a biscuit and looked at it. "My Anna made biscuits?"

Eyes wide, Anna nodded.

Kat watched Logan with his daughter and she wondered if the man sitting across from her had a brother, an evil identical twin who had fired her two days ago, then irritably rehired and brought her back here today.

He winked at Anna and Kat felt her own insides do a flip. Though she hardly knew him, Kat suspected that this side of Logan Kincaid—the teasing, smiling charmer—was a side that few saw, a side that emerged only for Anna. Kat knew that for Anna—only Anna—Logan had swallowed his pride and brought her back here. Anna wasn't happy, Logan had told her. He'd made it plain that he didn't feel she was right for the job and that he didn't want her here.

And yet, sometimes, Kat thought there was something in Logan's eyes, a look that she felt more than actually saw, a look that she understood more on an instinctual, rather than conscious level; a look of sheer masculine hunger that made every feminine receptor within her scream out a warning. She'd come to Texas for adventure and romance, but romance of a spiritual nature, not in a physical, sexual sense. And when it came to Logan, Kat had no doubt that's all there would be, the physical. The man radiated sex, and while she couldn't deny she was attracted, she also couldn't deny he terrified her.

To Anna's delight, Logan made a great show of eating three more biscuits, then after dinner insisted on clearing the table and doing the dishes while Kat helped Anna into the bathtub. After she'd bathed and dried off, Kat dusted

Anna with scented powder she'd brought from New York. Anna was still smiling when Kat helped her into bed.

"Do you really know how to play the violin?" Anna asked when Kat tucked the pink comforter around her.

Kat smiled. "Yes."

"Miss Carver, my nanny when I was six, before Mrs. Lacey came, she played the violin, too, but she was so bad that Daddy wouldn't let her play when he was home. The screeching gave him a headache."

One more reason for Logan to resent her being here, Kat thought with a silent sigh. "Thanks for the warning. I'll be very careful not to screech when your daddy's around."

"Miss Carver taught me to play a little, too," Anna said shyly. "And Miss Goodhouse, the music teacher at Harmony Elementary said I was very good."

Harmony Elementary? Kat had assumed that Anna had always had home tutoring. "When did you go to school in Harmony?" Kat asked.

"She went for one semester in the third grade."

Kat turned at the sound of Logan's voice. He stood in the doorway, his shoulders stiff, the smile he'd had earlier gone. So the evil twin was back, she thought with a quiet sigh.

"We'll go over Anna's lessons and schedule in a few minutes," he said, moving into the room. "I made some coffee, help yourself."

Kat was bright enough to know when she was being dismissed. She said good-night to Anna, then went to search for a mug in the kitchen. She never drank coffee, but she needed something to hold onto when she and Logan went over Anna's lessons. She dumped in milk and sugar, hoping to hide the taste, but when she sipped the hot liquid she wrinkled her nose at the still-bitter flavor.

She was sitting at the kitchen table when he came in a few minutes later. He poured himself a cup of coffee, then turned and leaned back against the counter.

"We haven't had a chance to talk about Anna yet," he said, holding her gaze. "About her disability."

Kat had the distinct feeling he'd expected her to look away when he'd used the word "disability." She knew there were people, a lot of people, uncomfortable being around, or even discussing the disabled. Based on his blank expression and flat voice, Kat had the feeling Logan himself wasn't comfortable.

"She was the most beautiful baby I'd ever seen," he said quietly. "A little button nose, big blue eyes, pink cheeks. Everything about her was perfect. She said her first word when she was ten months, took her first step when she was a year." He stared at his coffee cup for a moment, then finally continued. "JoAnn—Anna's mother—and I didn't really notice any problems until Anna was almost four. She just seemed lazier than normal, sometimes even refusing to walk, or crying if we made her. She couldn't seem to keep her balance and oftentimes she'd stumble or fall. When we took her into a specialist in Houston, he found a tumor in her spine. He operated, but there was nerve damage to the spinal cord that affected her lower body movement. She has partial feeling in her legs, but no motor control."

Kat tried to picture Anna at four, all the doctors and the hospital, the surgery. How scared she must have been. "And she's been in a wheelchair since then?"

He nodded. "We tried braces and crutches, but Anna, despite her soft-spoken nature, is quite stubborn, and wanted no part of it."

Kat had a good idea where Anna's stubbornness came from. The soft-spokenness must have come from her mother. "But surely, between your wife and yourself you could have—"

"My wife was never around." The bitter tone in Logan's voice cut through the silence of the room. "She decided she wanted to continue with her singing career and started accepting jobs anywhere she could find them, leaving Anna with a nanny or Sophia. The jobs got longer and longer, until finally she just didn't come home at all."

"She left her own child?" Kat asked in disbelief.

"She couldn't deal with the reality of Anna's illness, or the hard work. Running away was her way of handling a difficult situation. She was killed when the bus she was touring in hit an ice patch on a highway in Ohio and went off the road."

"I—I'm so sorry."

Logan shrugged. "Like I told you before, I didn't give a damn for me. It's Anna who took it hard, blamed herself because her mother left."

"Anna thought it was *her* fault?"

"I tried to tell her that it had nothing to do with her or her illness, that her mother left because she wanted to be a singer, but I know she never believed me. Anna used to say if she was like other little girls, her mommy never would have left."

How could a four-year-old possibly understand her mother leaving, when Kat herself didn't? Logan had every right to be bitter and angry. Kat hadn't even known the woman, and she was furious.

"JoAnn had no family, and my parents are both gone now. It's just been Anna and me for almost six years. She doesn't deal well with changes, so I've tried to give her stability in her life."

"Is that why you haven't remarried?" Kat wanted to kick herself the second the question slipped out. She'd forgotten this was her employer she was talking to, not a friend. "I—I'm sorry," she said quickly. "That's none of my business."

"That's only one of the reasons." He took a sip of coffee and stared at her over the rim of his cup. "Nor do I bring women here to the ranch. And since you've brought this up, I'd like to say that the same goes for you and whatever men you might meet while you're here. What you do on your own time, away from the ranch, is your business, but I won't tolerate any—" he hesitated "—*dates* here at the house."

Kat felt the hot rise of a blush on her cheeks, but she also felt the rise of irritation. What the hell did he think she was going to do, bring men here and take them into her bedroom? "I think I can manage to control myself," she said curtly.

"It's very important to me that Anna stay with a schedule and keep up her lessons, even in the summer," he went on as if they'd simply been discussing the color of the paint on the kitchen walls. "Mrs. Lacey left a curriculum. You can pick up where she left off."

"I saw the curriculum." It was dry and boring, but Kat was sure she could spark a little life into it. "I noticed there was no time set for art and music."

"Anna's going to need an emphasis on academics in order to help her move into the mainstream one day and give her more opportunities," Logan said flatly.

"Are you saying you don't want me to instruct Anna in the fine arts?"

He took a sip of coffee, his expression patronizing as he gazed down at her. "I see no reason for it. As a career, there's no future in it."

No future in it? She would have loved to show him her last year's tax return. "Why do you assume that? Anna is extremely bright and capable. She can do anything she wants to do."

Impatience twitched at the corner of his mouth. "Her life is going to be difficult enough with her disability. I don't want to encourage a job that's unsteady and unpredictable, with a high chance for failure."

"Studying music is not encouraging anything," Kat said with exasperation. "I'm only suggesting expanding her lessons to include a little music and art, that's all. Even Anna expressed an interest earlier. She said she'd been in a music class at Harmony Elementary and her teacher said she was good."

He stiffened. "Putting her in the local school was a mistake. And that music class was an even bigger mistake. Even now, two years later, every time that teacher sees me, she still harps on having Anna in her band. And every time

I tell her the same thing. Anna is not going to sit on a stage and have a lot of people stare at her."

"The only reason anyone would stare at Anna is because she's beautiful," Kat insisted.

Logan's mouth thinned. "Tell that to a crying child who's been laughed at because she dropped her instrument and couldn't pick it up."

The image brought a tightening in Kat's chest. "I know children can be cruel, but Anna is older now. Music might be a way to help build her confidence and feel good about herself."

"She can listen to appropriate music, and have hobbies, but the stronger her education in useful subjects, the easier it will be for her to find a place for herself someday outside this ranch."

Useful subjects? She set her back teeth, struggling not to tell him exactly what she thought of his ignorant, short-sighted ideas. "Even the most pedantic education allows for music and art, Logan. You can't really believe that force-feeding academics will help Anna adjust better as an adult."

His face darkened. "I've never forced anything on my daughter."

Kat knew she should back off, not only because Logan was Anna's father and it was his business how he raised her, but because he was getting angry.

But this was *music* they were talking about. Her passion, her life. And a life without music was unthinkable to Kat.

"Music and art will broaden Anna's education," Kat insisted, "put balance in her life and give her more choices."

"Like *your* choices?" Logan said tightly. "Whether to be a nanny or a waitress?"

She stared at him without blinking, without moving, then very slowly stood, coffee cup in hand and moved toward him. His face was like granite, his gaze dark and intense. Careful not to brush against him, she emptied her coffee into the sink and rinsed it.

"Good night," she said stiffly. When she turned to leave, he reached out and took hold of her arm.

"I shouldn't have said that."

She looked down at his hand on her arm, then lifted her gaze to his. "You know what you are, Logan Kincaid? You're a snob."

If she hadn't been so angry, she might have laughed at the sudden surprise in his eyes.

"I didn't mean to insult you," he said, his voice softer. "I only want what's best for Anna."

She supposed that was as close to an apology as a woman might get from Logan. He might be bullheaded and unreasonable, but he loved Anna fiercely, Kat was absolutely certain of that. And unless she wanted to go back to filling coffee cups and wiping down tables, she'd better learn to keep her opinions to herself.

She sighed and shook her head. "Anna is your daughter. I have no right to interfere. I'll follow Mrs. Lacey's course schedule, and comply with whatever else you want from me."

Kat watched Logan's eyes darken. As she realized what she'd said, she felt her face burn with embarrassment. His hand still rested on her arm, and her sudden awareness of the contact between them sent a shiver of electricity through her entire body. The tension between them stretched as taut as a wire and as dark as the night outside.

"When it comes to Anna, of course," she added, but she heard the breathlessness in her own voice and her embarrassment only deepened.

His hand slowly slipped away, but his gaze didn't. "Of course."

She prayed he didn't notice that her knees were shaking as she walked away. She stopped at the doorway and threw him a glance over her shoulder. "Oh, and one more thing, Logan."

He looked at her.

"I was a damn good waitress."

She didn't look back, just walked through the door, but she could have sworn she heard him laugh.

Four

At breakfast the following morning, the coffee was weak, the bacon burnt and the potatoes salty. Kat had scrambled the eggs, Logan noted, though not intentionally. Still, they tasted all right, and all in all it wasn't a bad meal. Even Anna had eaten. In fact, she'd not only cleaned her plate, she'd also cleared her place and hurried to get ready for her lessons. That was downright amazing.

But no more amazing than the woman sitting across from him, wearing a little cotton blue print dress, sipping at her own coffee as she chatted easily about the people she'd met in Harmony. When he'd asked her to cook for him, he hadn't considered that she'd be eating with him. Every nanny he'd brought in for Anna had always taken her meals into her room. All these years he and Anna had eaten quietly by themselves, which was exactly the way he'd liked it.

And now, here was Kat Delaney, a green-eyed bubble of energy and enthusiasm, sitting at his kitchen table as if she belonged there. After he'd insulted her last night, he'd expected the cold shoulder this morning. Whenever JoAnn had been angry at him—which was most of the time—she wouldn't speak to him for days. Either Kat hid her anger well, or she didn't stay mad long.

At the moment she was relating an argument in the café between Clifford Riggs, the town sheriff, and Stubbs, over who had caught the bigger trout in Sam's Creek. Logan really wasn't listening to what she was saying, as much as how she said it. She had a grace about her, something in the way she spoke and moved, that fascinated him. Her eyes were lighted, her movements animated and he found himself dawdling over the rest of his breakfast, something he never did. Breakfast and lunch he normally ate on the run, or carried in a sack out on the ranch. He never lingered after a meal, not with eight hundred head of cattle and fifty thousand acres of land to tend.

''...so when Clifford told Stubbs to stuff it,'' Kat said, ''Stubbs thought he was talking about him, not the fish, and two ranch hands from the Baxter place had to hold Stubbs back before he went after Clifford.''

She laughed at her own story, and the sound almost had a musical quality about it that had Logan smiling, as well. It surprised him that she'd met so many people in town in the two days she'd been there, and remembered their names, too.

Reluctantly he pushed away from the table and reached for his hat on the rack by the back door. Kat stood and began stacking plates.

''Anna has a checkup with the dentist at one forty-five,'' he said. ''I meant to tell you last night, but it slipped my mind. I won't be back in for lunch today, but she's easy to get in and out of the station wagon. It's parked behind the barn, and the keys are hanging by the back door.''

She dropped a knife and it landed on the floor with a loud clatter. He turned to look at her. She bent stiffly to pick up the knife, then stood and slowly lifted her gaze to his.

He narrowed his eyes. ''What?''

She caught her lower lip in her teeth, and the small, innocent gesture made his pulse jump.

"I...should have mentioned it...it just never dawned on me...in New York, it really isn't important, or necessary..."

Logan knew he wasn't going to like whatever it was she was trying to say. She hesitated and it dawned on him.

"Are you trying to tell me you can't drive?"

She shook her head. "There's never been any reason to learn. I've lived in New York all my life and transportation has never been a problem. I never thought about you needing me to drive Anna anywhere."

"You're twenty-four years old, Kat," he said with more exasperation than he intended. "How could you possibly have never learned to cook *or* drive?"

She straightened. "How did you know I'd never cooked before?"

He couldn't help the laugh. "Two things. Last night's meal and this morning's."

He cursed his words the minute they were out. She stiffened, and he saw the hurt in her eyes. *Damn his fool tongue.* He felt as if he'd just plucked the wings off a butterfly.

"Well, Mr. Kincaid," she said, her voice even. "It seems that once again I don't quite meet your expectations. So what exactly are you going to do with me?"

She stood in the middle of the kitchen, her legs long and bare, her hair a mass of curls that was pulled away from her face with a black headband, emphasizing her high cheeks and big green eyes. Unbidden, he felt a surge of desire sweep through him.

What exactly are you going to do with me?

A very good question, he thought, drawing in a deep breath, thankful that for once he didn't say the first thing on his mind, which was that he'd like to take her to his bed and keep her there for the next two months. She was Anna's nanny, for God's sake. He had no business fantasizing about this woman.

He sighed silently. She couldn't cook, she couldn't drive and they'd already argued over Anna's curriculum.

What next? he thought, then decided he really didn't want to know.

"Sophia will be here at noon today." He jammed his hat on his head. "She'll drive her."

Kat watched Logan turn sharply and walk out the back door. She slumped back down in a kitchen chair and closed her eyes.

How could I have been so stupid?

She should have considered that he'd want her to drive. Everybody drove. She'd thought about lessons for years, but somehow there'd just never been time, and between her parents and Max and Ollie, there'd never been a reason. Other than New York City, she'd never gone anywhere by herself before.

She was educated, she'd traveled, but outside of her career, what life did she have? She'd argued with Logan about putting balance in Anna's life, and she realized that she had none of her own.

But at least she was making an effort, she thought, sitting up straight. Wasn't that why she'd come here? To try new things and experience a different way of life? Since she was a little girl she'd wondered what it was like living in the West on a ranch, with horses and cowboys and all this incredible open land. Maybe she hadn't thought everything through carefully when she'd applied for this job, but she could be a good teacher and nanny to Anna. She knew she could.

"Is something wrong?"

Kat looked up and saw Anna in the doorway. It amazed her how quickly and quietly the child got around in her wheelchair.

"No." Kat forced a smile, then stood and gathered the rest of the dishes. "I'll just be a minute here and we'll get started."

"No one ever tells me the truth," she said softly, backing out of the room.

There was pain in Anna's quiet statement. Kat not only heard it, but she also felt it. She practically dropped the dishes in the sink and hurried to block Anna's way. "I'm sorry, Anna. You're right. I am upset."

Fear leapt into Anna's eyes. "Did my daddy fire you again?"

"No, sweetie, he didn't." *Not yet, anyway.*

"Then why are you upset?"

Kat took Anna's hands, then knelt beside her. "It's myself I'm upset with. Your daddy asked me to drive you into town for your dentist appointment today, and I had to tell him that I couldn't take you because I can't drive."

"You don't know how to drive?" Anna asked in astonishment.

Kat shook her head. "Pretty silly, huh?"

Anna sat up straight in her chair, her mouth set with determination. "You can learn. You're not too old. Mrs. Lacey drives and she's *old*."

Smiling, Kat squeezed Anna's hands. "Of course I can learn. And as soon as I get back to New York, I will. In the meantime, your daddy said that Sophia will drive you, okay?"

Anna nodded. "Okay."

"And speaking of learning—" Kat stood and playfully pinched Anna's nose "—if I don't want your daddy mad at me, I better get these dishes done and start your lessons. I'll rinse and you load."

Anna's eyes widened. "You want me to help?"

There was no sarcasm or argument in Anna's voice, just complete disbelief, the same disbelief that Kat had seen yesterday when she'd asked Anna to make the biscuits.

"Of course I want you to help." Kat turned on the water and grabbed a dishrag.

Anna almost looked frightened. "But I don't know how."

"Well, you can learn, can't you? Gosh, *I* know how, and look how old I am."

Anna giggled, then lined her wheelchair up with the open

dishwasher. "What are we going to make for dinner to-night?"

Kat wanted to say reservations, but this wasn't New York. There were no pizza deliveries, no Chinese takeouts. She had to admit she was still smarting from Logan's criticism of her cooking skills, but in all fairness, how could she blame him? The meat last night had been a little tough—okay, a *lot* tough, she amended, and the breakfast today less than marginal. She realized his critique of her expertise in the kitchen had not been intentional, but rather a slip of the tongue.

She wondered how to prepare tongue, even smiled as she imagined the look on Logan's face if she served him the unsavory dish. She quickly dismissed the idea, deciding instead that for some reason she couldn't understand, it was suddenly very important to her to impress and please Logan.

But how could she? Cookbooks might as well be in a foreign language, and based on what Logan had told her about Sophia's cooking, Kat knew she couldn't ask the housekeeper for help.

There was only one person who could help her. Kat knew it was a long shot to even ask, but what choice did she have? There was nothing she could do about her driving now, but she was going to learn how to cook if it killed her.

And Logan, too, she thought with a determined lift of her chin. That man was not only going to eat her meals, but he was going to eat his words, as well.

Logan had ridden out on horseback after breakfast, but after finding a downed fence in the north section, decided to come back to the house for his truck and tools. He'd intentionally waited until he was sure that Anna and Kat had gone into town with Sophia. He had no desire to taste leather by sticking his foot in his mouth again.

He'd felt like a heel all day. A first-class, five-star, tail end of a mule.

She'd looked so vulnerable this morning, with her big, innocent eyes and soft, pouty mouth. She'd been chatting cheerfully, and he had to go and pop her little bubble of enthusiasm.

Frowning, he opened the refrigerator and pulled out some lunch meat. Dammit, anyway, he thought, slapping a piece of turkey between two pieces of bread, this was *his* house, wasn't it? She worked for him, didn't she? So why did he feel like an ogre every time he opened his mouth around the woman?

He heard the voice then, a soft, feminine laugh coming from the other room. He moved to the kitchen door and listened, then heard it again. He couldn't make out the words, but it was definitely a woman's voice.

Kat?

Quietly he moved into the living room. He saw her sitting on an Indian print rug beside the couch, her legs folded tightly under her in a way that both fascinated and made him wince at the same time. Her back was to him, her hair falling forward as she bent over, scribbling in a notebook. He realized she was on the phone, and the receiver was tucked under her chin.

"No, I am not coming back," she was saying, "and there's nothing you can say to change my mind." She was quiet for a moment, then, "You're just going to have to deal with it, Oliver. I'm perfectly all right here, Anna is wonderful, and Mr. Kincaid has been..."

There was a long pause and Logan realized he was holding his breath.

"...the perfect gentleman," she finished, though Logan felt the word somewhat forced. He narrowed his eyes and leaned back against the wall.

Who the hell was she talking to? A boyfriend? He listened to her continue to argue with the man—Oliver—and it was quite clear he wanted her to come home, and it was equally clear she didn't want to.

A lover's quarrel? he wondered. Was she running away

from someone? Is that why she'd come here, and why she refused to go back home?

He knew he shouldn't be eavesdropping, that listening to private conversations was less than "gentlemanly," but they both knew he was no gentleman. And besides, he told himself, she was taking care of Anna. As far as he was concerned, that gave him certain rights.

"Ollie, please don't worry about me. I'm fine. Really. Two months will go by quickly and we can—"

She stopped suddenly, then turned and saw him. Her eyes widened and she slowly straightened. "I'll call you back later...yes—" she glanced at her watch "—seven o'clock, your time."

She hung up the phone, closed her notebook, then finger-combed her hair back away from her suddenly pale face. "I didn't hear you come in. I thought you weren't coming back for lunch."

Obviously. "I thought you were going into town with Anna and Sophia."

He watched as she unfolded those long legs of hers and stood. She'd changed into a white blouse, jeans and a pair of tennis shoes, he noticed.

"Sophia needed to pick up some lumber for her husband in town so she took her son to help her. Since she drove her truck, there was no room for me."

He took a bite of sandwich and nodded to the phone. "You didn't have to hang up."

"I was finished," she said simply, offering no other explanation.

Logan frowned. He'd been fishing, but she hadn't taken the bait. She held her notebook closely to her, making him wonder what she'd written in it. He was certain it was none of his business, but that didn't make him any less curious.

The silence stretched taut between them, and the quiet made Logan realize how very alone they were.

"I just came back for the truck." He pushed away from the wall and turned back to the kitchen. He needed to get out of here.

"Logan?"

He stopped and glanced back at her.

"Can I, uh, come with you?"

She wanted to come with him? Surprised, he simply stared at her.

"I promise I'll be quiet as a bird and stay out of your way and I won't even try to feed you."

The sassy smile that touched her lips made Logan's gut tighten. The last thing he wanted to do was take her with him, but what man could say no to a woman with that eager look in her eyes?

He turned sharply and headed for the back door. "I'll wait for you in the truck."

The Kincaid ranch was fifty thousand acres of rolling hills and wooded valleys. Yellow and purple wildflowers dotted the landscape and swayed in the afternoon breeze, while cattle grazed not far from the fence posthole that Logan was presently digging.

Kat stood under the shade of a large oak, listening to the sound of water bubbling over the rocks in the creek below and the chatter of birds overhead. The day was pleasantly warm, the air cleaner and sweeter than anything she'd ever breathed.

"Hey—" Logan took off his hat and ran the back of his gloved hand over his temple "—bring me that white bucket from the back of my truck, will you?"

It was the first time he'd actually spoken to her, and Kat jumped at the opportunity to help. The bucket, filled with tools and assorted nails, was heavy, but using both hands, she managed to bring it to him. He laid the shovel aside and took the bucket from her as if it weighed no more than a feather.

Since she'd now been invited, Kat stayed, hands behind her back while she watched Logan lift a large fence post and maneuver it into the hole he'd dug. The muscles in his back and arms rippled and strained against the sweat-drenched chambray shirt he'd rolled to his elbows.

She'd never watched a man work like this before, had never seen such pure masculine power. She felt odd, light-headed even, and glanced quickly away.

"The shovel," he grunted, dropping the post in place.

She grabbed the tool and handed it to him, trying not to notice the iron strength in his sinewy arms, or the way his skin glistened with moisture.

But she did notice. In fact, she was outright staring, much to her embarrassment. Admittedly her experience with men was limited, but she had never felt such overpowering, knock-the-breath-out-of-you lust for anyone before. But, of course, she'd never met anyone like Logan before. Maybe all cowboys exuded the same virility, she told herself. Or maybe it was the myth, the legend of the West she was enamored with, and any slow-talking Texan in a cowboy hat and boots would have the same effect on her.

Except that she'd already met several ranch hands when she was working for Stubbs. They'd all talked slow, worn hats and boots, and not one of the men had made her knees wobble or her breath catch.

"You better get out of the sun," she heard Logan say. "Your face is all red."

She touched her hands to her cheeks and felt the heat of her own skin. Mumbling something incoherent, she turned and walked back to a shady part of the creek where she splashed some cold water on her face and neck, careful not to look at Logan again.

Had he seen her gawking at him? she wondered. She didn't think so; he'd thought she'd just had too much sun. Still, she felt like an idiot, losing her composure that way. She was attracted to him, she certainly wouldn't deny that, but to openly ogle the man was inexcusable. If the tabloids had seen her look at a man that way, they'd be lovers by the next edition.

Lovers. The thought was like a hot whisper on her neck, and she quickly pushed it out of her mind. She wasn't interested in a summer fling; she'd come here to get away, to be someone different for a little while before she was on stage for two years. When her tour was finished she'd find someone and settle down, have babies. She leaned back against a rock on the creek's edge and closed her eyes. Babies. A family. The thought made her smile.

"You okay?"

Her eyes flew open at the sound of Logan's voice. He stood over her, his hat tipped back, his expression concerned as he stared down at her.

"I'm fine," she said, averting her gaze from the pair of strong, denim-clad legs in front of her.

He knelt beside her, scooped up a handful of creek water to splash his face, then drew another fistful to his lips. Mesmerized, Kat felt her own lips part as she watched Logan drink the cool water. She started to lean toward him before she caught herself.

Knees bent, legs out in front of him, he sat beside her, tipped his hat forward, then tucked his hands behind his neck and closed his eyes as he lay back on the cool ground.

She waited a few moments, but he seemed to have forgotten she was there. "It's beautiful here," she said, but he did not respond.

With a sigh, she leaned back against the rock, not caring if she was talking to herself. "I sent away for some tourist literature before I came here, but no picture could ever capture this sense of peace or tranquillity."

Eyes still closed, Logan gave a short, dry laugh. "Just wait until the next thunderstorm or tornado hits and see how peaceful it is."

So he *was* listening. "But it's that very drama," she insisted, "that uncertain, powerful force of nature that adds to the beauty and excitement."

He cracked one eye open. "It's not beautiful to see the roof lifted off your barn or hailstones the size of baseballs kill twenty head of cattle."

"Of course it's not." She sighed with exasperation. "But don't you just accept that as part of what you do, and doesn't all this—" she swept her arm out "—and knowing that you're a part of it make up for the tragedy or disappointments?''

He had both eyes open now. ''What movies have you been watching? Ranching is hard work and long hours, and just one of those little 'dramas,' as you called them, can wipe out a lifetime of work in the course of five minutes.''

''But you still do it.''

''It's what I've always done, what I'll always do.''

''But you don't like it?''

''Of course I like it.'' There was an edge of irritation to his voice. ''I love it. Why the hell else would I be doing it if I didn't?''

She smiled sweetly. ''So it's hard work, unpredictable and the chance for failure is always there, but you wouldn't do anything else because you love it, right? Sort of like a career in the music or art field.''

Logan closed his eyes and groaned silently as he remembered those were nearly his exact words to her last night regarding the fine arts. She'd set him up, and he'd swallowed whole the hook she'd baited.

''All right, Miss Delaney, you win.'' With a heavy sigh, he sat and tipped his hat back to look at her. ''Anna can have music lessons, but only after her other lessons are done.''

She smiled brightly, and he almost felt as if his surrender was worth it. Damn but if the woman wasn't already getting under his skin.

''John Wayne,'' she said.

''John Wayne?'' He'd expected a thank-you, or maybe a long speech about how he wouldn't be sorry. John Wayne he hadn't expected.

''You asked me a minute ago what movies I'd been watching. John Wayne.''

He shook his head, trying his damnedest to figure this woman out. Every time they seemed to be moving in one direction, she suddenly veered off in another.

She picked a yellow wildflower and twirled it between her fingers. ''I'm an only child, but when I was ten or eleven I had an older cousin who always brought a John Wayne movie to watch when he came over to visit. Dmitri used to stick one hip out, strut around and in his best John Wayne voice say, 'Well, pilgrim, looks like we got trouble.'"

"Dmitri?"

"My family is Russian. My father was a factory worker in Moscow, my mother a seamstress. They came to America a year before I was born and started their own company." She paused, then went on. "Anyway, Dmitri sort of got me hooked on Westerns, but I had to sneak watching them. My parents disapproved."

"Your parents disapproved of John Wayne?"

She smiled at Logan's surprise. "My teachers convinced my parents that movies with cowboys and horses and shootouts were frivolous."

"Is that why you applied for this job?" Logan frowned at her. "To satisfy a childhood fantasy about the Wild West?"

She tossed the flower into the creek and watched it float away. "Partly. I've lived in New York all my life. It's an exciting city, full of energy and fascinating people. But I've always wondered what it was like to live in a small town, to experience a slower pace and be close to nature."

As if in response, a nearby cow mooed. Logan watched Kat stare dreamily across the land he'd learned to take for granted. The sky was a deep blue today, the hills still green from an early summer rain. She was right. It was beautiful here. It had been a long time since he'd noticed.

But the landscape wasn't the only view he noticed. He watched Kat lift her hair off her neck, tilting her head to catch a breeze. There was a graceful fluidity in the way she moved, and the heat he suddenly felt had nothing to do with the temperature of the air and everything to do with the way her long, slender fingers sifted through her shiny hair. He had an overwhelming, almost painful desire to replace her fingers with his own and feel those silky strands against his palms.

"I realize that coming here was impulsive, but it's a dream come true for me, an opportunity I might never have again." She turned toward him and her green eyes shone with excitement. "Don't you think that if you truly feel passionate about something you should just do it? Not think about it, not analyze it, but just do it, damn the consequences?"

She'd leaned close to him and the feminine scent of her skin encircled him as if it were an invisible net. His gaze dropped to her mouth, and the sight of her soft, enticing lips were his undoing.

So without thinking, without analysis, damn the consequences, he just did it.

Five
———

The second his mouth closed over hers, Logan knew he'd made a mistake.

A big one.

He felt her surprised intake of breath, then the warmth of her soft parted lips. She started to say something, and he took advantage of the opportunity to deepen the kiss. He explored the silky sweetness of her mouth, savoring the taste and texture as if she were a fine wine. The want he'd felt only a moment ago turned to an aching need, but she sat perfectly still, not moving away, yet not responding, either.

Disappointment shot through him like a sharp knife. What had he expected? For her to melt into his arms, or better yet, jump his bones? Whatever he'd expected, he was a damn fool.

He started to pull away when her hands cupped his face, holding his lips mere inches from hers. Her eyes opened slowly and he saw a mixture of amazement and confusion there.

Her eyes, a deep smoky green, held his, then, to his surprise, she slowly brought her mouth back to his. When she tentatively touched her tongue to his lips, he circled her waist with his hands and pulled her against him. She was softer and sweeter than he could have imagined, and when he felt her body tremble lightly, he had no more thoughts.

What was happening to her? Kat thought dimly. She'd been kissed before, for heaven's sake. But never, ever like *this,* never with such intensity, never with such hunger. Or was it just that she'd never responded to anyone like this before? Sensations rippled through her. Pleasure. Heat. Excitement. Wave after wave washed over her. She felt breathless and giddy, light-headed.

An urgency grew between them and his mouth turned hard, demanding. Her pulse pounded in her head, and she met his tongue with her own, shamelessly greedy for more. Her hands moved over his cheeks and jaw, his skin was hot and damp, and the light stubble of his beard against her soft fingertips sent electrical impulses coursing up her arms. Instinctively she strained closer to him and the press of her breasts against his chest aroused her even more. She wanted him to touch her there, she realized. She felt swollen and achy and the desire to feel his hands on her bare skin made her whimper with need.

Just do it. Kat's words pounded in Logan's head and through his entire body. Take her right here, on the creek bank, with the soft grass as a mattress and the sky as a ceiling. Damn the consequences. Her hands moved sensually over his face and neck, and her body pressed longingly against his. He dragged her closer to him, intending to roll her onto her back, strip those tight jeans, then—

He froze. What the hell was he thinking? He couldn't do this. Not with Kat. She was his daughter's nanny, for God's sake. They had to live together under the same roof for the next few weeks. If he gave in to his lust in a moment of weakness, it would create an impossible situation. Other than a warm bed for a few nights, he had nothing more to offer her. And in spite of her unexpected response to his kiss, he knew that she wasn't a roll-in-the-hay-and-then-forget-it kind of woman.

With a willpower he didn't know he possessed, Logan lifted his mouth from Kat's, then took hold of her arms and pulled away. She opened her eyes slowly and the smoldering passion he saw there nearly had him reaching for her again. Her lips were swollen and moist and he tightened his hold on her arms, struggling with his own desperate need to finish what he started.

"Kat," he said hoarsely, "I'm sorry."

Dazed, she knotted her brow in confusion. "You're sorry that you kissed me?"

Only because now he knew what she tasted like, what she felt like, and it wasn't enough. "I shouldn't have done that."

She frowned at him. "You shouldn't have?"

He shook his head. "We aren't children, Kat. A kiss like that would only lead to trouble."

"Oh." She seemed to think about that. "I never thought of making love as trouble. Is that what it means to you?"

He nearly choked at her words. She looked so damn innocent and serious at the same time, he wasn't sure whether to groan or laugh.

"Of course," she went on, "it would mean we'd have to get married right away."

His throat went dry. "What?"

"And big weddings certainly are a lot of trouble, aren't they? And then my parents coming for visits and spoiling all the kids. That's trouble, too. Or—"

"All right, Kat," he said tightly. "I get your point. Maybe trouble wasn't exactly the right word, but I think you know what I mean. It would be—" he paused, wanting to make sure he used a better word this time "—awkward."

"Forget about it, Logan." She stood and brushed the grass off her jeans. "It was just a kiss. You need to learn to lighten up a little."

Just a kiss? Lighten up? Stunned, he watched Kat walk

back to the truck, annoyed by her casual dismissal. In spite of himself, he couldn't help but admire the swing of her hips and the glint of sunlight off her shiny hair.

He rose and followed her to the truck. She was climbing into the cab when he caught up with her. He took hold of her hand and pulled her back down.

"What are you doing?" she asked as he dragged her around to the other side of the pickup.

He opened the driver door and leaned close to her. "I'm lightening up," he said huskily, pushing her back against the seat.

Her eyes opened wide. "You are?"

He nodded. "Put your hands on my shoulders."

When she hesitated, he did it for her, then slid his hands around her waist.

She laughed nervously. "Look, Logan, I was just—"

"You're way too stiff," he said tightening his hold on her waist. "Now loosen up and do everything I tell you."

She gasped as he lifted her suddenly and put her behind the wheel. He shut the door, walked around to the other side of the truck and got in.

"Now drive," he said and reached for his seat belt.

It was too nice a day to stay inside for Anna's lessons, so they'd dressed in shorts and T-shirts and sat comfortably on a blanket under the shade of an oak not far from the barn. Anna had told Kat that Mrs. Lacey was allergic to dust and horses, so they had always stayed inside. Anna had described Mrs. Lacey's condition in animated detail, right down to the puffy face, red blotches and explosive sneezing, making Kat wonder why the poor woman stayed here at all.

No doubt the nanny had fallen in love with Anna, too, Kat thought. With her soft gray eyes and sweet smile, the little girl had captured Kat's heart completely. As each day passed, the thought of leaving her, of leaving here, became more difficult.

More than a week had passed since Logan had kissed

her by the creek. They'd eaten breakfast and dinner together every day, had casual conversations over the weather or Anna. He'd even given her driving lessons around the ranch after dinner. But he hadn't looked at her once the way he'd looked at her just before he'd kissed her. He hadn't shown any interest beyond what was for dinner, or how Anna had done. Based on Logan's indifference to her, she was beginning to wonder if maybe she'd dreamed him kissing her, if the encounter was simply a figment of her imagination.

But then she'd remember the feel of his lips on hers, the touch of his hands on her body and she knew she hadn't dreamed it.

The logical side of her brain told her that she should be embarrassed at the way she'd thrown herself at him, but for some strange reason, she wasn't. Kissing Logan was the most natural, the most thrilling experience of her life. Telling him that it was "just a kiss," had to be the greatest performance of her life. She still didn't know how she'd managed to walk back to the truck on legs that felt like melted rubber.

She sighed and combed her hair away from her face. Maybe it had been "just a kiss" to him, after all. She'd told him to forget about it, and apparently he had. But she certainly couldn't, and she wasn't going to mitigate that experience with guilt or worry or shame, either. That kiss was going to have to last her a very long time, through at least two years of travel and performing, perhaps much longer before she ever met another man like Logan who turned her inside out and upside down. She wanted to remember every exquisite detail.

At least he couldn't complain about her cooking anymore. Oliver's daily and detailed instructions had slowly improved the palatability of the meals. Logan hadn't said anything, of course, but she'd seen the surprise on his face over a week ago when he'd bit into her first attempt, Rosemary Chicken à la Oliver. She'd been just as surprised. It tasted wonderful. Since then, she and Anna had made spaghetti, three kinds of chicken, beef stew with dumplings and an apple pie that Logan had nearly eaten by himself.

But in spite of Logan's aloofness, there was an anxiety in the air. An uneasiness that left her unsettled. A tension in her seemed to stretch as each day went by. She wasn't sure how long it would be before she snapped.

"I'm done."

Anna handed Kat the paper she'd been working on, a short essay on the life of Beethoven.

Getting Logan to change his mind about instructing Anna in the fine arts had been Kat's greatest triumph. She was still amazed that he'd given in, but she wasn't going to question it. They'd started with music history and Anna seemed to enjoy her new lessons. She'd even asked to write the report on Beethoven after Kat had told her that the composer had written some of his greatest symphonies after he'd gone deaf.

She started to read the paper when Tom drove up and honked. He waved, then parked the truck and walked over, followed by an ebony-haired little girl wearing glasses.

"You remember my niece, Julie, don't you, Anna?" The foreman's white smile flashed against his dark skin. "You girls went to the same school for a little while."

Anna nodded shyly.

"My daddy said I could come and help my uncle Tommy groom the horses today," Julie said to Anna. "You wanna help, too?"

Anna looked at Kat, and the frightened expression in her eyes made Kat's chest ache.

"We'll all help," Kat said quickly, then jumped up to lift Anna into her chair.

Julie walked beside Anna, chatting all the way to the barn about the upcoming Blue Grass Festival in Southcreek, another small town not far from Harmony. Anna was quiet, but seemed to be listening intently to Julie's account of last year's festival.

In the barn, Julie handed Kat and Anna a brush while Tom brought out a chestnut mare.

"This here's Stardust." Tom secured the horse to a post.

"When is her baby due?" Kat asked. She'd never been around horses before, but it didn't take an expert to notice the mare's bulging stomach.

"Not for a few weeks." Tom ran a hand over the horse's back. "She's a good little cow horse. Logan's hoping her foal will be like his or her mommy."

Tom brought out a second horse, a black gelding named Pepper. Anna and Julie brushed the horses' legs while Kat and Tom brushed the backs and rear. Anna talked easily with Julie now and seemed to relax as she grew accustomed to her task.

Tom threw a saddle on the gelding when they were done and Kat watched while he buckled and cinched everything.

"Ever been on a horse?" Tom eyed Kat's legs, then adjusted the stirrups.

"Good heavens, no," Kat said with a laugh. "I'm still working on a driver's license."

"No time like the present."

"Oh, no, I couldn't, I mean, I can't—" Her protest turned to a small shriek as Tom suddenly had her foot in his hand, then boosted her up and in the saddle.

Kat's heart lodged in her throat. She was so high! Breath held, she grabbed tightly onto the saddle horn. "He's so big," she said in a high-pitched voice.

Tom grinned up at her. "Don't let that scare you, Kat. No matter what the size, just hold on and don't take any guff."

"Easy for you to say." Kat had always loved horses, but her mother had been terrified of them and had never allowed any riding or lessons, no matter how much Kat had begged when she was little. If her mother saw her now, Kat knew she'd probably faint.

When Pepper dropped his head suddenly and shook his mane, Kat squeaked loudly.

Julie and Anna burst into giggles, and Kat realized it was the first time she'd ever truly seen Anna laugh. The sound filled Kat with pleasure. She'd sit on an elephant, she decided, if it made Anna happy.

Kat held onto the saddle horn while Tom held the reins and walked her around the inside of the barn.

"Okay, Miss Anna Funny Pants—" Kat reached for Tom's hand when they stopped, then brought her leg around and slid off the horse "—your turn."

Anna stopped laughing immediately. There was a mixture of fear and excitement in her eyes as she looked from Kat to the horse. "But I can't..."

"Of course you can," Kat encouraged. "Tom can lift you up, and we'll both be right here."

Anna's lips parted as if she wanted to speak, but no words came out.

"You can do it," Julie said eagerly.

Tom lifted Anna from her chair and set her sideways on the saddle. Kat stood beside Anna, while Tom moved to the other side of the horse.

"You're riding!" Julie exclaimed.

Anna's cheeks flushed pink and her eyes sparkled. The bright smile on her face made Kat's heart stir.

"What the hell is going on here!"

Kat turned at the sound of Logan's booming voice. He stood at the entrance to the barn, hands on his hips.

"Nothing's going on," Kat started to explain. "Anna's just—"

"Get her off that horse." Logan moved toward the animal, his face tight with anger, his arms stiffly at his sides.

But he moved too quickly, and Pepper started at the unexpected motion. The horse tossed his head up and stepped sideways, throwing Anna off balance. She cried out and started to slip from the saddle when Logan grabbed hold of her and pulled her into his arms.

Logan's face was a controlled mask of fury as he gently set Anna back into her chair. "Are you okay?" he asked his daughter.

She nodded, her skin pale now and her lips trembling.

Logan straightened and looked at Kat. "In my office. Now."

Kat watched Logan storm off without giving her a chance to say a thing. Stunned, she looked at Tom.

"He'll calm down," the foreman said.

Kat sighed heavily, then knelt down beside Anna. "I'm going to go talk to your daddy, sweetheart, then I'll be right back. Why don't you and Julie finish brushing Stardust?"

Anna's face was red as she glanced at Julie. Julie picked up the brushes and handed one to Anna, then, as if nothing had ever happened, continued the conversation she and Anna had been having about Julie's roller-coaster ride at the amusement park in Arlington.

Kat looked at Tom again. "I'll be right back. Can you keep an eye on things here?"

He grinned at her. "Sure thing."

She took a deep breath, turned on her heel and headed for the house.

Logan waited for her inside, pacing behind his big oak desk, his teeth clenched tight and his hat pulled low on his head.

His rage dulled to a heavy anger. What had the woman been thinking? Obviously she hadn't been thinking at all. Why else would she have done something as stupid as putting his daughter on a horse?

His anger crowded out everything else he'd been thinking before he'd walked into the barn, like Kat's incredibly sweet lips, her soft green eyes, that sexy sway of her hips. He'd been going crazy for the past few days with thoughts of her, ever since he'd kissed her by the creek.

And the nights. Lord help him, the nights had nearly done him in. More than one morning he'd found his sheets torn up and his body dripping in sweat. Other than meals and the driving lessons, which he told himself were necessary, he'd done everything to keep away from her.

And he intended to continue to stay away from her, too. But first, he was going to make a few things perfectly clear with her. Namely that she was never to put Anna on a horse again. Then he'd talk to his foreman, too. Tom knew that Anna didn't ride, that she couldn't ride. What the hell was the matter with him?

The door to his office flew open. Kat walked in, then keeping her gaze carefully locked on Logan, closed the door tightly behind her.

"What the *hell* is the matter with you?" she said, her voice low and furious.

What the hell was the matter with him? Logan frowned darkly. This wasn't how this conversation was supposed to start. Her eyes were spitting green fire as she crossed the room.

"Now just you wait a minute—"

"No, *you* wait." She moved around the desk and stood in front of him, her arms folded. "What were you thinking, coming into the barn like that and scaring that horse while Anna was sitting on him? Haven't you got a brain in your head?"

He couldn't believe what she was saying. *She* was yelling at *him?* Momentarily stunned, all he could do was stare.

"And in front of a friend, Logan." She spun sharply away, then threw out her hands and turned back to face him. "How could you?"

"How could *I?*" He finally choked out the question. How in the hell had this discussion turned into what *he'd* done wrong? "Anna can't ride. Even to a city girl, that should be pretty obvious."

"She wasn't *riding,* for heaven's sake, she was *sitting.* And she was having *fun,* something she doesn't do very often. If you hadn't come in there like a bull with a bee on its butt, Mr. Logan Kincaid, that would have been pretty obvious even to *you.*"

Kat heard her own words, but she couldn't believe she was actually saying them. She'd intended to reason with Logan, calm him down, but with every step she'd taken toward the house, all she could see was the look of embarrassment on Anna's face, all she could think about was that Anna might actually have been hurt. Reason and logic flew out the window, and a slow, burning anger came in the front door.

His jaw tightly clenched, Logan stared at Kat. Tension sparked between them as they faced each other, nose to nose, eye to eye. A library clock ticked from the office wall. Sophia hummed in the kitchen.

And then there was another sound. A child's laughter from outside.

Kat held Logan's dark gaze. "When was the last time you heard that sound, Logan?" she asked quietly.

His eyes narrowed, then he turned slowly and went to the window. She moved beside him and looked out.

Julie had pushed Anna beside the corral where Tom was exercising Pepper on a lead line. Both girls were waving at the horse every time it came around, and the animal would fling its head up and shake its mane. Each time the girls would break into giggles.

"I know how much you love Anna," Kat said gently. "And I understand why you're afraid for her. Every parent wants to protect their child."

He stared out the window. "Anna's different from other children."

She shook her head. "Why? Because she can't walk? That makes her special, not different. She wants to have friends, wear the same clothes, go to parties. Do all the same things that other kids do."

He stiffened. "She can't—"

Kat put her hand on Logan's arm. "Stop thinking about what Anna *can't* do, and start thinking about what she *can* do. Let her know that you believe in her, that you know she can do anything. Her disability doesn't have to stop her from doing anything, or being anything she wants to be."

Logan said nothing, just watched as Tom brought Pepper by the fence where the girls were and gave them each a carrot to feed the horse. Anna held hers out stiffly, then laughed with delight after the animal muzzled it away.

"I didn't even know she liked horses," Logan said thoughtfully. "Mrs. Lacey said that the flies and smells were too much for a child as delicate as Anna, that the dust and hay made her sneeze.''

Kat would very much like to give Anna's regular nanny a piece of her mind. But what good would it do? The woman would be back in a few weeks, and Kat knew that she'd be on her way to Europe after her opening performance in New York.

The thought left an empty hole in Kat's stomach. She realized that her hand had tightened on Logan's arm. She felt the iron strength of his muscles under her fingers and the heat of his skin through his white cotton shirt. He looked down at her, and when his eyes met hers the hole in her stomach turned into a knot.

''Anna's not as delicate as you think, Logan,'' she said, letting her hand slip away. ''She's a very bright, very strong little girl. More than anything, just remember that, and let her be a little girl. Trust me, she'll be grown up soon enough.''

She stepped away from him, then left.

Logan watched her close the door behind her, then turned his attention back to his daughter. Tom's niece was turning Anna in circles and they were both laughing. He couldn't remember how long it had been since he'd seen her play like this. Not since she was very little, before her surgery. He'd tried to find friends for her, he'd even tried the elementary school. But when those kids had laughed at her and he'd seen tears in her eyes, he swore he'd never let anyone hurt her again.

Maybe Kat was right. Maybe he had missed some of Anna's needs, needs that had nothing to do with education or physical well-being.

And as he continued to watch his daughter play and saw her smile, a strange feeling permeated his chest, sort of like a balloon slowly filling.

He suddenly realized that he was smiling, too.

Six

Kat pulled the meat loaf and potatoes out of the oven and set the food she'd been keeping warm on the counter. She stared at the clock over the oven door and sighed. It was already eight. Logan obviously wasn't coming home for dinner.

Why hadn't he at least called? she thought, wrapping the food in foil, then putting it in the refrigerator. After she'd walked out of his office earlier and gone back outside with Anna and Julie, she'd seen him talking to Tom by the barn. Then he'd gotten in his truck and left without saying a word to her. He still hadn't come back.

This time he was going to fire her for sure.

She couldn't believe she'd said all those things to him. *Haven't you got a brain in your head?* And where in the world had she come up with *bull with a bee on its butt?* She groaned every time she recalled her words.

In her mind, she could hear her cousin Dmitri saying, "Well, pilgrim, looks like we got trouble."

In spite of what most people thought about temperamental artists, she'd never been petulant or subject to childish outbursts. Every emotion she'd ever felt—anger, fear, joy—she'd channeled into her violin and her performances. Discipline and control were important to her, in her work, as well as her life.

Maybe that was her problem. She hadn't even picked up her violin in over two weeks. What else would explain her losing control with Logan as she had? She'd actually *yelled* at him, for heaven's sake. Well, raised her voice, anyway. To her, that was yelling. What was it about the man that brought out such extreme emotions in her? Of course, the fact that he was stubborn, close-minded and inflexible might certainly contribute to her anxiety whenever he was around, but she'd been around lots of men like that and had never lost her temper before.

No, Logan wasn't like any man she'd ever met. Not even close. The rough texture of his voice, the strong cut of his jaw, the dark intensity of his eyes. Everything about him brought her senses to life, made her feel as if she'd been turned inside out and her nerves exposed. Even his scent, a mixture of man and leather, made her pulse skip.

The faint sound of a violin playing drifted from Anna's room, a recording that Kat had given her, Kreisler's Praeludium and Allegro. Anna had played it over and over, and told Kat that this was going to be the first piece she was going to play. Kat hadn't wanted to discourage Anna, so she hadn't told her that it was much too difficult for her. It would take a lot more than a few months with a school band to learn a piece that complicated. Kat had planned on working with Anna to learn a few simple pieces before she left, but now, after what had happened this afternoon, they might not even have time for "Mary Had a Little Lamb."

Disappointment settled in the pit of her stomach like a lead weight. She'd miss Anna terribly. In just two short weeks she'd grown extremely fond of the child, and she knew Anna felt the same way about her. It would not be an easy goodbye.

Still in a daze, her mind on Logan coming home and

firing her, Kat walked to Anna's room to tell her it was time to get ready for bed. She knocked lightly at Anna's door, but there was no answer, just the sound of a mournful violin. Kat's thoughts had been too distant to really listen before, but she listened now, turning on her trained ear as she stood outside the door.

Something was wrong, she thought with a frown. This wasn't the recording she'd given Anna. It was very close, but not exact. Confused, Kat opened the door and looked in.

She froze.

It was *Anna* playing.

Her jaw went slack as she stared. How could this be? *Anna* was playing a complicated piece that most advanced students couldn't play. And she was playing it well. Better than well.

Shocked, Kat watched her. The child hadn't noticed her yet and Kat studied her movements, the way she fingered the instrument, her timing. She was a little tentative, but she played beautifully.

If Anna could play like this naturally, with so few lessons, what would she be like under the guidance of a teacher, another virtuoso?

Someone like herself.

Did Logan have any idea that his daughter was musically gifted? she wondered. No, he couldn't know, she told herself. Surely he would have encouraged Anna, however he might feel about music being frivolous. What parent would intentionally hold back a child with this kind of ability?

Mesmerized, Kat couldn't move; all she could do was stare and listen as Anna continued to play, lost in her own world. Kat understood that feeling of being swept away, a state of concentration so intense that nothing else existed. Prodigies like this were rare, and the thrill of discovery sent excitement racing through her.

She couldn't wait to tell Logan. He had to come home sometime. She'd wait for him all night, if necessary.

Kat moved into the room, hating to disturb Anna's playing, but too eager to stop herself. "Anna?"

Anna's hands stilled and the room went silent. She set the violin and bow down, then bit her bottom lip and looked at Kat timidly.

"Sweetheart, where did you learn to play like that?" Kat knelt beside Anna's wheelchair and looked up at her.

"Was it okay?" Her expression was hopeful.

Okay? Good heavens, even Anna had no idea how good she was, Kat realized. "Yes, sweetheart, it was much better than okay. It was wonderful."

Anna smiled. "I've been practicing all week, every time you went driving with my dad. I wanted to surprise you."

"I *am* surprised." More than she could imagine, Kat thought. "Does anybody know you can play?"

"I used to play a little in the afternoons, but Mrs. Lacey gets headaches, so I had to stop."

Kat thought she might actually strangle the woman if they ever met. The very thought of that woman coming back here sent chills up Kat's spine. Whether it was her business or not, Kat was going to speak to Logan about the nanny.

"Do you think you can talk my dad into letting you give me lessons?" Anna asked hesitantly. "I mean, if you think I'm good enough."

If she was good enough! Kat was only sorry that they'd already wasted two weeks.

After she tucked Anna into bed Kat went into the living room and waited, trying to think of the best way to tell a stubborn, hardheaded rancher that his daughter was a musical genius.

The house was dark when Logan came in close to eleven. He closed the back door quietly behind him, afraid he might disturb Anna or Kat, but the truth be known, what he really wanted to do was wake up the entire household.

He couldn't wait to see Anna's—or Kat's—expression when they saw the gifts he'd brought.

With an excitement that surprised even himself, Logan made his way through the kitchen and went into the living room. He hesitated, and for one crazy moment he actually did consider waking everyone up.

He'd hoped to be back by dinner, but Tanner McGee was as slow as molasses. If Logan didn't know that the man's work was the best in all of East Texas, maybe in the entire state, he would have gone elsewhere. But there were times when only the best would do, and this was definitely one of those times.

He looked at the saddle he'd carried into the house and smiled. Anna's saddle.

At first, when Logan had brought in the new saddle and asked Tanner to customize it for him right away, the man had flatly refused. But after Logan told the custom leather worker exactly what he wanted and that it was for Anna, there hadn't been another word of complaint. In fact, he stopped smack dab in the middle of fitting George Bruner for new boots, told three other people waiting to come back tomorrow, then put up his closed sign and went to work on the saddle Logan had brought.

The result was nothing short of spectacular.

Still smiling, he was halfway through the living room when he realized a lamp had been left turned on to a low setting. He also realized a second later that Kat was lying on the sofa, sound asleep.

Had she waited up for him? he wondered. He noticed the book on the couch beside her. Or had she simply fallen asleep reading?

Quietly he set the saddle and the bag he carried down on the floor, then moved beside her. The soft light spilled over her delicate features; shadows emphasized her high cheeks, her hair fell around her face in a dark curtain that shimmered with red and gold. She looked peaceful and relaxed now, unlike the tigress who had burst into his office earlier, ready to pounce on him for threatening her cub.

The name Kat fit her well, he decided. She had the sleek curves and moved with the grace of a feline, and when she was riled, her claws came out and her eyes narrowed with catlike precision.

Did she think of Anna as her cub? he wondered. It had certainly seemed so this afternoon. Mrs. Lacey was efficient and competent, but he'd never had the feeling that the woman was anything more than a caretaker for his daughter, and he knew that Mrs. Lacey would *never* have argued, or even questioned him when it came to Anna, even if she thought he was wrong.

Kat, on the other hand, was ready to scratch his eyes out because she'd thought that he'd endangered Anna's safety and embarrassed her in front of a friend.

He smiled, remembering the sound of Anna's laughter this afternoon when she'd played with Julie. She needed friends, activities outside of the ranch. Kat had made him realize that.

But Kat had also made him realize other things. Things that he'd denied not only Anna, but himself: a woman's touch. Not only in the carnal sense, but in other, intangible ways. A feminine presence, the kind of warmth that filled a house and made it a home. The smile she greeted him with when he came in at the end of the day, the new recipes she tried, the sound of her humming while she helped Anna get ready for bed.

He'd even enjoyed teaching her to drive. His smile widened as he thought of that first time he'd put her behind the wheel of his truck. That lesson had reminded him of his first ride on a bronc. Wild and exciting. Out of control.

Exactly what he'd felt when he'd kissed her.

He'd worked hard at forcing that kiss from his mind, but as he looked down at her now, he let himself remember. Her lips had been soft and sweet, her body warm and pliant against his. In his mind, he could still hear that little moan she'd made when he'd deepened the kiss, and even now his body instantly responded.

Against his better judgment, he allowed his gaze to slowly move over her, taking in the curve of her hip and the soft rise and fall of her breasts under the thin floral wrapper she wore. Her knees were bent slightly, allowing only the tips of her bare feet to peek out from the bottom of her robe.

He had the craziest need to slide his hand over those bare feet and continue up her long, sleek legs all the way to—

"Logan?"

He nearly jumped at the sound of his name. Her eyes, heavy with sleep, were watching him. *Dammit.* He felt as if she'd caught him peeping through her window.

She rose on one elbow, parting the deep slash of her robe to reveal the swell of her breasts. He tore his eyes away, certain that Kat Delaney was his punishment for every bad thing he'd ever done in his life.

"I didn't hear you come in," she said, her voice low and husky. She sat, combing her hair away from her face with her fingers, without realizing that when she raised her arms she'd only widened the V of her robe, exposing more flesh and the lacy top of some feminine night wear.

Damn, damn, damn.

He had to swallow before he could speak. "Why aren't you in bed?"

"I wanted to talk to you."

Talk was the last thing on his mind right now. What *was* on his mind required no words at all. "It's late, Kat."

She looked at the slim gold watch on her wrist and frowned. "It *is* late. Are you hungry?"

He was starving and it had nothing to do with food. He did realize, though, that in his excitement with Anna's saddle, he hadn't eaten, nor had he thought to call. He suddenly felt guilty.

"I'm fine. I should have called."

"It doesn't matter," she said, but somehow he felt that it *did* matter, and strangely enough, the idea that it mattered to her, mattered to him.

He watched with a mixture of relief and disappointment as she pulled her robe tighter around her. He didn't dare sit next to her, so he stood, forcing her to look up at him.

"I want to apologize," she said quietly. "For the way I acted earlier."

Giving or receiving apologies had always made Logan uncomfortable. "Forget it."

She shook her head. "I shouldn't have said those things."

He was starting to feel annoyed. Where was the sassy little spitfire who had stood up to him earlier? "I said, forget it."

"It wasn't my place to talk to you like that, Logan, I—"

"Have you changed your mind about what you said?" he asked.

She said nothing, just stared at him, her lips pressed tightly together.

"I didn't think so. So why are you apologizing for telling me what you think?"

She lifted her chin and held his gaze. "I don't want you to fire me."

"You think I'd fire you because you care more about my daughter than agreeing with me?"

Relief loosened her shoulders and softened her eyes. "I yelled at you, Logan. I never yell."

"You call that yelling?" Without thinking he sat down beside her. "Darlin', a newborn pup has a louder bark than you."

She folded her arms indignantly. "I can't believe you're making me feel inferior because I don't yell loud enough."

Shaking his head, he laughed. "I didn't say I *wanted* you to yell, did I?" His laughter died and the smile that had been on his lips faded. "God only knows, Anna heard enough of that when JoAnn was here."

There was a weariness in Logan's voice that almost had Kat reaching for him. He raised his daughter alone, and she knew that was the way he wanted it. But there had to be times, she reasoned, when even the most determined loner needed to talk.

"Had you known her a long time before you were married?" she asked.

He shook his head and leaned back on the couch. "I met her when she was singing at a bar in Dallas. She could belt out a tune like nobody I'd ever heard. I knew she wanted a singing career, that she craved the spotlight, but I was only twenty-three and in love. I talked her into marrying me and a year later we had Anna."

He paused for a moment, and Kat saw a small smile lift the corners of his lips. "Bringing Anna home from the hospital after she was born was like a little miracle all wrapped up in a pink blanket. Even JoAnn seemed to settle down and everything was pretty good for the next couple of years." His smile faded. "Then she wanted to start singing again. She'd leave Anna with Sophia at the drop of a hat if she got a call for a gig somewhere. That's when the fights between us started, and for the next couple of years it was rough. I wanted her to stay home for Anna, but after Anna's surgery, JoAnn left for good. She wrote once in a while and told Anna she'd be back, but JoAnn and I both knew that was a lie."

A hard glint shone in his dark eyes. "Anna asked about her mother constantly for the first year, then she never asked again. She didn't even cry when I told her that JoAnn had died. It was as if I was talking about a stranger."

Kat closed her eyes, not sure if she could speak through the thickness in her throat. When she did speak, all she could manage was a whisper. "She has you, Logan. In spite of everything, I'd say that makes her one lucky little girl."

There was surprise in his eyes at her words, then amusement. "So you don't still think I haven't got a brain in my head?"

Embarrassment burned Kat's cheeks. "I'm sorry, I never should have—"

"Kat." He took her chin in his hand. "I'm teasing."

Logan Kincaid teasing? Kat saw the upward curve of his lips, then smiled herself.

"So tell me," he said lightly, "have you ever actually seen a bull with a bee on its butt?"

She felt her blush deepen. "I have a vivid imagination."

"Do you?" His gaze dropped to her mouth.

Kat's heart skipped, then raced. The air surrounding them grew heavier, darker, pulling her into a world of heightened senses. He'd leaned closer, bringing with him the male scent of his skin and the heat of his body. His voice was rough and deep, his breath warm on her neck.

When he'd kissed her before, at the creek, he'd been rough, his mouth demanding and forceful. This time, his lips barely brushed hers, a mere whisper of a touch, but the effect was every bit as powerful and exciting as the first time. No, more so, she decided, much more so. She could barely breathe; her heart pounded in her chest. She shuddered from the force of it.

And when he pulled away, she fought the urge to drag him back.

"Thank you," he said, his voice heavy and rough.

"Thank you?" It was difficult enough to speak, let alone understand the words.

"For being here for Anna, for putting a smile on her face and laughter in her voice." He hesitated, and for one brief moment she almost thought he might kiss her again. "I put her in an ivory tower to protect her. I never thought I might actually be hurting her."

"You'd never hurt her," Kat said softly.

He shook his head. "I have hurt her. And maybe I can't change what I've done, or haven't done in the past, but today and tomorrow I can do something about."

Grinning, he reached into his pocket. "Starting with tickets to the Blue Grass Festival in two weeks."

"Logan!" Kat stared at the tickets he waved under her nose. "How did you know?"

"I saw Tom and Julie in town this evening. After I apologized to Julie for being so grumpy, Tom mentioned the girls had been talking about it. You told me Anna likes music, so I thought this might be a good place to start."

She stared at Logan for a long moment. *Anna and music.* She'd nearly forgotten. She swallowed hard, trying to think of an easy way to tell him about Anna's incredible talent.

After all he'd told her about his ex-wife, she could only imagine how he'd take to the news that his daughter was a musical prodigy.

Before she could say a word, he stood suddenly, bringing her with him. He took her hand and pulled her around the couch to where a saddle lay on the floor. It had a big pink bow on it.

"It's for Anna," he said. "I bought it for her in town tonight and had it customized with special stirrups. I thought maybe I could teach her how to ride."

She didn't even know what to say. Kat knelt beside the saddle. That's where he'd been all afternoon and night, she realized. Having a saddle made for Anna.

"It's beautiful," she whispered, running her hands over the smooth leather. "Oh, Logan, I'm so sorry."

"Sorry?"

She looked up at him. "I thought you'd been gone all night because you were looking for my replacement. I spent the entire night trying to think of how to talk you out of firing me."

His smile was lascivious as he held out a hand to help her up. "Damn. I wish I would have known that before. We could have 'talked'—" he wiggled his eyebrows "—a lot longer."

Amazed at this playful side of Logan, Kat just shook her head and smiled.

He still held her hand, even though she was standing now. "I bought you something, too."

"Me?" A present from Logan? Kat heard the breathless, excited tone in her own voice.

He let loose of her hand and handed her a large white plastic bag with a big box inside. Her hands were shaking when she laid the box on the couch and opened it.

Boots. He'd bought her a pair of brown embossed boots with a silver buckle on the instep.

They were beautiful.

"I thought you could use something more practical than

the shoes you've been wearing,'' he said awkwardly. ''You can exchange them if they don't fit.''

''They're perfect.'' She touched the buckle, then ran her fingers over the delicate designs on the brand-new leather. It was the most wonderful present she'd ever been given. She looked up at him, but she was too overcome with emotion to speak. ''Thank you'' was all she could manage.

Kat looked at the tickets in Logan's hand, the saddle on the floor, the boots he'd given her and she realized how far he'd come in one day.

There were still things to talk about. She knew she had to tell him about Anna, but there was no reason he had to know tonight. She'd wait, and when the time was right, she'd tell him. Once he heard his daughter play, Kat was sure Logan was going to be as thrilled as she was.

Seven

"**T**urn left here and park between those two boulders under that tree."

Kat checked her side and rear mirrors, flipped on her turn signal, then turned off the main highway onto a dirt road. She felt and heard the crunch of gravel under the truck's tires as she carefully pulled the pickup into the spot Logan had indicated. He got out of the truck after she parked, then gave her the okay sign on a good job.

They'd been working on parking and backing up today and she'd only run over one curb in town, and that was only because everyone in Stubbs's café, including Stubbs, had come out to watch her. She'd been so nervous she went right over a cement divider. Several of the men who'd been watching offered their own suggestions on learning to drive, which only erupted into an argument between Stubbs and the sheriff over the proper way to parallel park. They'd been yelling so loud at each other, they hadn't even noticed when she'd driven away and knocked over Stubbs's stand-up sign in front his restaurant.

Still, all in all, she'd done very well considering she'd only had a few lessons. She drove around the ranch by herself now, but when she went out on the road and into traffic, Logan always went with her. Between her driving and Anna's riding lessons, Logan never had a moment to spare.

It had been a week since the night he'd brought home Anna's saddle. She'd been thrilled, and she'd had her first lesson that same morning after breakfast. It was a daily routine now, one that Anna looked forward to, along with the violin lessons in the afternoon. It amazed Kat how the little girl had flourished emotionally and physically, as well. Her confidence, as well as her legs, seemed to be gaining strength with each passing day. Julie came over often, also, and had invited Anna to a slumber party after the Blue Grass Festival. Logan had said no, maybe next time, but Kat knew that he was nervous because Anna had never spent the night away. The girls hadn't given up, though, and had been working on him to change his mind.

Kat still hadn't told Logan about Anna's music ability. There'd been so many changes already, and she was afraid if she pushed too hard too soon, he might throw the walls back up again. Soon, she knew. It had to be soon.

When she realized she couldn't see Logan outside the truck anymore, Kat shut off the engine and slid out of the cab. As her feet touched the soft dirt, Kat couldn't help but admire the new boots Logan had given her. Each time she wore them, which was often, they felt more comfortable, as if they were made only for her. She liked them so much, she even bought Oliver a pair and sent them to him as a thank-you for helping her learn how to cook long-distance.

She moved around to the back of the truck and saw Logan kneeling on the ground beside the right rear tire.

"Something wrong?" she asked.

"We picked up a piece of glass somewhere." He stood and reached into the back of the pickup for the jack. "We're losing too much air to make it back to the ranch. I'll have to change the tire here."

"Can I help?"

He frowned at her. "Call me a chauvinist if you want, but as long as I'm around, you won't be changing a tire."

As long as I'm around. Why did those words create such a strange mixture of longing and disappointment inside of her? She sighed quietly, knowing full well the reason why. Because he wasn't going to be around much longer. Because *she* wasn't going to be around much longer.

Kat sat on one of the boulders beside the truck and took advantage of the opportunity to watch Logan work. He'd rolled the sleeves of his white shirt to his elbows and the ripple of muscle in his arms and shoulders fascinated her. She went to bed at night thinking of that strong, powerful body and couldn't help but wonder what it might feel like against her own.

She'd admitted to herself, from the first time she'd met him even, that she was attracted to Logan. And while she wasn't exactly a woman of the world, she wasn't a child, either. She understood the lure of physical desire. It was a natural, completely normal response between the sexes. He was a handsome, rugged man, she was a young, healthy woman. They were sharing a house and meals. It was perfectly understandable she might be curious what it would be like to share his bed, also. What woman wouldn't?

And yet, it felt like much more than curiosity to her. Much more than simple interest or preoccupation. In fact, there was nothing simple about her feelings at all. They were...deeper. More intense than anything she'd ever experienced.

And those feelings, if she let them get out of control, were going to bring her nothing but a broken heart. There was nowhere for those feelings to go, she knew. Her life right now, with her music and her tour, was wrapped up neatly, complete with ribbon and bow. It was what she wanted. What she'd always wanted.

Wasn't it?

With a sigh, she rose and moved to the edge of the bluff overlooking the canyon. The sun was starting to go down, and the sky was a palette of yellows and oranges over the distant mountaintops. She watched the colors deepen, then slowly change to reds and golds. The breeze danced and whistled in the treetops and the sound of rustling leaves filled the evening air. She knew that no matter what she did, no matter where she went, she would always remember this place and this moment.

When Logan walked up behind her a few minutes later he found her staring at the horizon, her hands linked behind her back. His breath caught at the sight of her standing at the edge of the bluff with a riot of color as her backdrop and her hair loose and tumbling around her shoulders.

He moved closer, but she didn't seem to notice him, so deep were her thoughts. He couldn't help but wonder what those thoughts were, and if maybe he was anywhere in her musings. Without thinking, he started to reach for her, then quickly pulled his hand back.

She noticed the movement and turned to glance over her shoulder at him. Her eyes were soft and dreamy looking.

"Like it?" Logan waved a hand toward the canyon.

She smiled and turned back around. "I think it's the most beautiful thing I've ever seen."

He thought she was the most beautiful thing he'd ever seen. "This is the back part of my property," he said casually.

Eyes wide, she turned to look at him again. "All this is yours?"

He nodded. "It's harder to get to, so I rarely even see it, and never from up here."

"It's incredible," she said softly, watching the sun sink behind the mountains. She shivered when the breeze picked up.

"Cold?"

"A little." She hugged her arms to her. "But I'm all right."

He leaned close to her, thinking of several ways he could warm her. But he didn't touch her, not only because his hands were dirty from changing the tire, but because he knew if he did, he'd kiss her. And from previous experience, he also knew if he kissed her now, with the sun setting behind them and with no one around for miles, he wouldn't be able to stop.

"I could stay right here forever," she whispered.

Could she? he wondered. And he wasn't just thinking about this spot. He was thinking about Harmony.

No. He almost laughed at the thought. She was city, he was country. And in spite of all the romantic notions, the two rarely mixed. She'd come here to experience a different way of life, and he knew that she'd enjoyed being here, in spite of their rocky beginning. But that didn't change who she was or where she came from. When it was time to go back to New York, she'd pack her things, and all this, Anna and the ranch, and Logan Kincaid, would be a distant memory.

He'd been there before and he had no intention of going back.

"You haven't ever mentioned what you were going to do when you go home." He'd avoided the subject of what she was going to do after she left here, but suddenly he felt more than curious. He felt as if he needed to know.

Her shoulders stiffened slightly. "I...I'm part of an orchestra," she said simply. "We have a tour coming up in the fall."

An orchestra. A tour. What could possibly be farther from his life-style? He'd never really given a lot of thought to Kat's life or what she did outside of the ranch. It hadn't mattered to him before and now—

He sighed. Now it didn't matter, either. It would be an interesting summer with her around and when she left, his life and Anna's life would be back to normal. Not that he knew what normal was anymore.

"We better get back." He walked back to the truck and climbed in on the passenger side. She got in behind the driver's wheel and started the car.

"By the way," he said, hooking his seat belt. "Sophia's

going to stay with Anna tomorrow afternoon while you're gone."

"Gone?" She flipped on the truck's headlights and looked at him. "Where will I be?"

He leaned back in the seat and tipped his hat forward. "Taking your driver's test."

The scent of barbecue and chili peppers seasoned the late-afternoon air of the annual Fourth of July Blue Grass Festival in Southcreek, Texas. Red, white and blue streamers decorated the carnival booths and bandstands, and the lively sound of banjos and fiddles poured from every corner, encouraging old and young alike to grab a partner—friend or stranger—and dance along. Fascinated, Kat stood at the back of the crowd, listening to a high-spirited number by a group called the "The Blues Boys." Several couples two-stepped by her and through the throng of surrounding people while line-dance enthusiasts designated their own space to kick and spin on the side.

Music, Kat knew, had the ability to inspire, and no matter what the bands played—jazz, blue grass or country—the dancers adapted and followed along without missing a beat. Inspired herself, Kat bounced to the music, pausing to wave at Tom who had taken Anna and Julie up to the front row to watch the band while Kat waited for Logan to return with drinks for the girls. Tom waved back, then turned to talk to a pretty redhead who had walked up and laid her hand on his shoulder.

Leaning back against a wooden fence post, Kat searched the sea of cowboy hats for one particular black Stetson that stood taller than most.

It was impossible to stop the small smile that touched her lips as she thought of Logan. She'd been doing that a lot lately. Thinking of him, then smiling.

She was too old to have a crush on a man, for heaven's sake. She nearly laughed at the absurdity of the thought. Infatuations were for teenagers, not mature, responsible adults.

''Hey, you think you could wake up long enough to give me a hand here?''

Caught daydreaming, Kat felt the rise of a blush as she looked up at Logan. He held three cones of cotton candy in one hand and a box filled with sodas in the other. Candy bars bulged out of the pocket of his blue chambray shirt and the front pockets of his blue jeans, and he'd tied three bright red balloons to his wrist. He also had a stuffed pig under one arm, and a teddy bear under the other.

So much for mature, responsible adults, she thought, giving him the hand he'd asked for by clapping.

''Very funny, Sleeping Beauty.'' He frowned, but his eyes smiled. ''Now how 'bout a little help before I smack you with my cotton candy.''

Laughing, Kat took the cotton candy and stuffed animals.

''I'll be back,'' he said, imitating Arnold Schwarzenegger. He hurried toward Anna and Julie, unloaded balloons, candy and soda, then came back for the stuffed animals and two cotton candies, leaving one with Kat. On his second return, he unexpectedly grabbed hold of a heavy-set, gray-haired woman and twirled her to the tune of ''Cotton Eyed Joe.''

Shaking her head at his antics, Kat watched Logan release the woman and tip his hat to her. He turned then, and Kat held her breath, thinking for one thrilling moment as he looked at her that he was going to dance right over to her and pull her into his arms. Instead he turned again and grabbed a skinny brunette in a bright yellow square-dance costume.

This was certainly a side of Logan she hadn't seen yet. Over the past two weeks, she'd seen subtle changes in him. He'd stayed a little longer at dinner, joked with Sophia. He hardly scowled at all anymore, and he'd even taken her and Anna out for a Congratulations lunch at Stubbs after she'd passed her driving test. When he'd announced her accomplishment to everyone in the café, they'd clapped and cheered and she'd bowed graciously, thinking she couldn't remember when applause had felt that good.

She watched as he let loose of the square dancer and made his way toward her. His blue shirt accentuated his broad chest and muscular arms, and his dress jeans and black boots were the image of virility. Her heart tripped at the sight of him, and she knew she wasn't the only female responding to Logan's masculinity. Several women watched him, one buxom blonde even wrapped her arms around his neck and stopped him to dance with her, though from the way the woman plastered herself against his body, she was thinking more of a Bedroom Mambo than a Texas Two-Step.

The flash of jealousy Kat suddenly felt surprised her. She had no business entertaining thoughts like that. She was his employee, Anna's nanny. She'd be leaving in a few weeks. She had no right to feel possessive, even if he had kissed her.

Even if she did want him to kiss her again.

And more.

The blonde slipped a piece of paper in the front pocket of Logan's jeans, then smiled seductively as he let loose of her and tipped his hat. Kat clenched her teeth and pretended great interest in her cotton candy when he moved beside her. He was too close, dammit. She could smell the musky scent of his aftershave and the faint odor of chocolate.

"I hope you realize that all that sugar you just gave Anna is going to have her wired all night," she said in the most proper tone she could manage.

"Won't be my problem." He pulled a chocolate bar from his shirt pocket and tore off the wrapper. "Or yours, either."

Kat watched Logan take a bite of the candy. "What do you mean?"

"I'm taking her and Julie over to the slumber party in a few minutes. There won't be room in the pickup for all of us, so Tom's going to take you back to the ranch."

It took a full heartbeat before his words sank in. "You mean you're actually letting Anna go to Julie's slumber party?"

"Sure. You have a problem with that?"

A problem? She almost threw her arms around him and kissed him. "Of course I don't have a problem with that. I think it's wonderful. You, on the other hand, are the one who said no the last two times Julie asked."

"Third time's a charm." He grinned and polished off the rest of the candy.

This was *definitely* a side of Logan she hadn't seen. In spite of the riding lessons and the fact that he'd allowed Anna music lessons, he still hadn't encouraged outside activities.

Maybe this was a good time to tell Logan about Anna. For the past two weeks, she'd been waiting for the right moment. Surely, with him in such a congenial mood, this had to be it.

"Logan," she began, but when she looked at him, she felt her throat close up as she watched him lick a spot of chocolate off his thumb. With a mind of their own, her lips parted and she had to stop herself before she leaned into him and pressed her mouth to his hand.

"Hmm?"

"Nothing," she said weakly. Tonight, she decided. She'd tell him tonight. When there'd be no distractions. Just the two of them.

Alone. Her heart stopped, then began to race. She and Logan were going to be alone.

She looked quickly away, drawing in a slow, deep breath to calm herself. They were going to be home alone. No one else.

So what? she scolded herself. That didn't mean anything. Did it?

No. Of course not. She was fantasizing. Fantasies based on nothing more than a couple of simple kisses and her own wild imagination.

And though she tried to force them from her mind, those fantasies slipped in. Logan kissing her, touching her, bare skin against bare skin...

"Having a good time?"

She nearly jumped at the sound of his deep voice so close to her ear. She could hardly tell him she'd been having a very good time—in her mind. "Yes," she answered a little too quickly. "Why wouldn't I be?"

"Barbecue and blue grass is a far cry from New York and classical music." Logan leaned back against the fence, wondering what had prompted the blush on Kat's cheeks. The breeze lifted the ends of her hair and carried her scent to him, a light, flowery fragrance that was as sexy as the white V-necked T-shirt she wore and the long, flowing lilac skirt. "I thought you'd be bored by now."

"Well, you thought wrong. I'm having a wonderful time."

Logan felt his stomach tighten as she plucked off a feathery ribbon of cotton candy and popped it into her mouth. "Even without Tiffany's and Tchaikovsky?"

"There's certainly more to my life than New York and classical music," she said with a touch of indignation.

"Is there?"

"Of course."

"Like what?"

"Like..." She paused, searching. "Like my friends."

"Like Oliver?"

She stopped in the act of peeling away another strip of cotton candy. "How do you know about Oliver?"

"I know that you call him almost every day, and that he wants you to come home." Logan leaned close. "Should I be worried about a jealous boyfriend showing up at my front door?"

"Oliver's not jealous," she blurted out.

She hadn't denied he was a boyfriend, Logan realized with a touch of annoyance. "Are you running away from him?" he asked. "Is that why you've come here?"

"Running away from Oliver?" Kat laughed, and the sound had a musical quality to it. "Of course not."

Still no denial. Logan frowned. "Then what are you running away from?"

"I'm not running away from anything, or anybody," she

said with exasperation. "I already told you why I came here. I've always wanted to experience ranch life. I'm between jobs, I saw your ad and I applied."

He regarded her for a long moment. The music had stopped for a moment, then started up again with a faster, bouncier beat. "Somehow, I don't see you as the impulsive type."

"Oh really?" Delicately she placed a bite of cotton candy into her mouth. "And I suppose you are?"

Logan's throat went dry as he watched Kat lick her finger. He could almost feel the soft spun sugar as it melted in her mouth.

That's when he knew he had to taste it, too. He had to taste her.

"Maybe I am," he murmured, then bent his head and took her mouth quickly, before she could protest. He felt her breath catch, then the rush of warm air as her lips parted.

Lord, but she was sweet. Incredibly, impossibly sweet. Her tongue met his, welcoming, her lips were soft and pliant under his. He wanted desperately to take her in his arms, to pull her against him and kiss her until she melted against him like the candy had melted in her mouth.

Dimly Logan heard the crowd cheering and clapping to a fiddle solo and the announcer calling out encouragement, but it was Kat that filled his senses, Kat that consumed him.

He pulled away, saw the flare of desire in her smoky green eyes as she opened them. Her lips were still parted and moist from his kiss, and it took every ounce of control he possessed not to drag her against him again.

"Chocolate cotton candy," he said softly.

She looked at him blankly.

"We just invented a new flavor of cotton candy. Chocolate. We'll make a million."

Shaking her head, she laughed softly and pushed a wad of the threadlike candy into his mouth.

"Logan Kincaid!"

Kat and Logan turned at the shrill call. A short-haired

brunette wearing thick glasses and a lace-collared Victorian print dress waved over the crowd and made her way toward them. Kat felt Logan stiffen as he watched the woman approach.

"Logan, hello." Out of breath, the woman pressed her hand to her chest while drawing in a lungful of air. "What a surprise to see you and Anna here."

Logan nodded at the woman. "Hello, Trudy."

Trudy pushed her glasses up her nose as she looked at Kat. "Hello." She offered a big-toothed smile and her hand. "I'm Trudy Goodhouse. Have we met?"

Kat shook her head and took the woman's hand. "Kat Delaney."

"You're Anna's nanny for the summer, aren't you?" Trudy asked. "Punch Wilkins told me you play the violin."

Kat shifted uncomfortably. The subject of her violin playing was one she'd rather avoid.

"I play a little myself," Trudy said. "Perhaps we could have a duet session sometime."

Kat hesitated. "Well, I really don't play—"

"Now, now, don't be shy," Trudy said brightly. "I'm no virtuoso myself, though I am proud to admit I received second place at the Austin Music competition last year for my rendition of Sarasate's Zigeunerweisen."

Kat's last compact disc had featured that piece and hit the top of the classical charts. "Congratulations. That's one of my favorites."

"Trudy's the music teacher at Harmony Elementary," Logan said tightly.

"Anna was in my class for a short time two years ago. I was extremely disappointed when she left." Trudy stopped and squinted closely at Kat. "Are you sure we haven't met? You look terribly familiar."

Apprehension fluttered in Kat's stomach. She forced a polite smile. "I'm certain I would have remembered."

Trudy stared at Kat for a moment longer, then gave her head a little shake. "Yes, well, I told Logan way back then that his daughter had a remarkable proclivity for music."

So someone *had* noticed Anna's talent, Kat realized. But did this woman know just *how* remarkable? She glanced at Logan and saw his jaw tighten. So much for his good mood, she thought with a silent sigh.

"Anyway, Logan," Trudy went on, "at least I'm glad to see you've finally come to your senses. Now that you're allowing Anna to play publicly, perhaps you'll call that conservatory in Dallas I told you about and—"

"What the *hell* are you talking about?" Logan straightened abruptly. "My daughter does not play publicly."

Flustered at the sharp tone in Logan's voice, Trudy hesitated. "But, she does, well, I mean, she is. Right now, as a matter of fact. Don't you hear her?"

Logan's head turned sharply and his face was like stone as he listened to the snappy beat of a fiddle accompanied by a harmonica. It was impossible to see the stage from where they stood, but it did indeed appear that the crowd had focused their attention on the spot where he'd left Anna with Julie and Tom only a few minutes ago.

Oh, no, not now...not like this, Kat thought. This was no way for Logan to find out about Anna. Heart pounding, she followed him as he made his way stiffly through the crowd. He stopped suddenly and went perfectly still as he saw his daughter at the foot of the stage, violin tucked under her chin, bow in hand, delighting the crowd as she played a brisk country tune.

Logan started toward her, but Kat took hold of his arm. "Logan, please, don't embarrass her. Let her finish and we'll talk about it later."

She felt his resistance, saw the determination in his eyes to snatch his daughter away from the people she entertained. His body was rigid, his lips pressed firmly together. She felt the battle waging inside him, then slowly, mercifully, he stopped, his gaze hard as he watched Anna play.

The child was amazing, Kat thought as she watched Anna play. She had the extraordinary ability to hear a piece of music, then play it herself with her own technique and interpretation. And even though Kat had heard Anna play several times now, she still was astonished at her ability.

When she finished, the crowd cheered wildly. Smiling, Anna handed the violin back to the boy who'd been playing before her and the band moved immediately into a new number.

Kat felt Logan take a deep breath, then walk calmly to Anna. Her cheeks were flushed and her eyes shone with excitement. Tom gave her a kiss on the cheek and Julie hugged her. Several people crowded around, complimenting her and shaking her hand.

"Did you see me, Daddy?" Anna asked as Logan moved beside her. "Did you?"

"Yes, sweetheart, I did. You were wonderful."

Anna beamed at her father's praise, but was too excited to see that there was no smile on his face as he wheeled her out of the crowd.

"That was too cool!" Julie said, dancing alongside Anna. "I can't wait to tell everybody at my slumber party tonight that you played with a real band. You'll be famous."

Kat saw Logan flinch at Julie's words. "Anna," he said evenly, "I think it's better if you stay—"

"Logan." Kat touched his arm. "Please."

A muscle twitched in Logan's eyes as he stared at her. She saw the anger in his eyes, but held his gaze, pleading silently with him to let Anna go to the party.

"Logan! Oh, Logan!" Trudy Goodhouse was pushing her way through the crowd like a football player heading for the end zone. "Wait up!"

"I'm going to take the girls over to Julie's now," he said tightly, ignoring the approaching woman. "I have a date tonight and I'll be home late. Don't bother to wait up for me."

Kat sank down into the dark, swirling water, letting the hot liquid bubbles work their magic on her tense body. Moonlight rippled in the surging water and reflected off the rising steam, while on the other side of the patio wall, crickets fiddled a staccato tune. Above her, the stars sparkled like night glitter.

I have a date. Don't bother to wait up for me. Ha! She folded her arms and lowered herself deeper into the rushing water. Why would she wait up for him? She wasn't his keeper. She wasn't anything to him, except an employee. He could stay out, *on his date,* all night if he wanted. What business was it of hers?

So why then, on the drive back to the ranch with Tom, through two chapters of a book, and three games of solitaire, had she been wondering what he was doing and who he was doing it with?

The blonde. The one who'd slipped him her phone number. What man could resist that kind of an offer from a woman who looked like that? And Logan was definitely a man, she thought, remembering the kiss he'd given her earlier at the festival. In spite of the hot water, she shivered at the thrill that ran through her.

Dammit, anyway. She had to stop thinking about him that way. It would lead to nothing but frustration. So he'd kissed her. So what? He'd kissed her before—one of those, "I'm curious" kind of kisses. It hadn't meant anything to him then, and it didn't mean anything today, either. He'd been relaxed, having a good time, and he forgot himself for a minute. She was making a big deal out of nothing.

With a sigh, she leaned her head back against the side of the spa and stretched her foot toward one of the pulsating jets. The problem was, to her it wasn't nothing. It was something. Very much something.

And since Logan was out on a *date,* he obviously didn't feel the same way.

Moisture burned her eyes. She was a fool to let him get under her skin. She was leaving in a month. She *had* to leave.

But what if she didn't? What if she stayed? If he wanted her to stay?

She closed her eyes and laughed. More fantasies. Fantasies as elusive as the steam rising around her. She couldn't stay if she wanted to—which she didn't. Even if he asked her to—which he wouldn't. Besides, she had a contract. She'd worked her entire life toward an opportunity like this. It might never come again.

She knew what she wanted. She'd always known what she wanted: to travel the world and play her violin. Love and family would wait. She wasn't about to let a few out-of-control hormones cloud her thinking.

Was she?

Logan stood at the edge of the spa, wondering what Kat had laughed softly about a moment ago. A smile still played on her enticing lips, and her eyes were closed.

She hadn't heard him open the sliding door from his bedroom and come out on the patio. He knew he should announce his presence, but even if it was only a few seconds, he wanted to look at her, to let his eyes feast on what his body denied him.

She'd piled her hair up on her head and it cascaded in damp ringlets around her oval face. Moonlight shimmered off the swirling water and her wet shoulders. His gaze followed one thin strap of her black bikini down to the swell of her breasts where water bubbled in the soft valleys and peaks, making him wish to God he was one of those bubbles. His pulse raced at the sight of her long, lithe body stretched out in the swirling water, and he felt an instant tightening in his groin.

She was beautiful. He'd known that from the first time he'd looked at her. She'd raised those gray-green eyes to his, smiled as she'd taken his hand, and he'd known right there that he wanted her.

He'd denied it, of course. Told himself that he'd brought her back only because of Anna, that he hadn't fired her half a dozen times after that because it would upset Anna. But it was all a lie. In his gut, he knew he'd kept her here for him. Because *he* wanted her. He'd always wanted her.

Even tonight, when he'd broken his date with Carol, he'd

told himself that he needed to come home and check on his mare and see if she was in labor. But that was a lie, too.

He'd fought his need for Kat, kept his distance, but he couldn't deny it any longer. Not to himself, not to her.

On a strangled curse, he reached for the top button of his shirt.

Eight

Vaguely Kat heard someone calling her name. She thought for a moment she was dreaming, that she had fallen asleep in the spa. But there it was again. Like a whisper of need, she heard Logan's distant voice calling her.

Confused, she opened her eyes. He wasn't distant at all. He was close. *In the spa.* She drew in a sharp breath and instinctively sank lower into the water.

"Logan," she said breathlessly. "I thought you, I mean, I didn't expect—"

"I didn't expect me, either." He dragged his wet hands through his hair and slicked the dark ends away from his face. "I thought you'd be at the festival until after the fireworks."

She could hardly tell Logan that after he'd told her he had a date, the festival wasn't fun anymore. "I asked Tom to bring me back early."

She watched as he sank into the water with a contented sigh, then leaned his head back against the brick edging of the spa. She felt practically naked in here with him, and the fact that they were all alone only increased her anxiety.

But maybe this was the opportunity she'd been waiting for, to talk to him about Anna. He seemed relaxed now, much calmer than earlier.

"Logan," she said after a moment of silence, "I'm sorry about what happened at the festival, with Anna, I mean. I had no idea anyone would ask her to play."

A muscle jumped in his jaw, but he said nothing.

She tried again. "She has a remarkable gift, Logan. I know how you feel about her playing the violin, but you can't deny she's wonderful. She is truly—"

"I know she's wonderful."

Kat hesitated. "Well then, now that you've heard her play and you know how amazing she is, you can understand how necessary it is to find the right teacher for her."

"I've heard her play before," he said flatly. "I already know she's amazing, and the only thing necessary is that she continue her education as it already is."

He already knew? She couldn't have understood him right. "Are you saying that you knew Anna was a prodigy?" she asked carefully.

"Of course I knew. She's my daughter. And the fact that I know, and have always known, doesn't change a thing. I don't want her playing publicly."

"I can't believe this." Kat sat up straight, then realized how little she wore and sank back down again. "She has a rare gift, Logan. You can't deny that."

"I'm not denying a thing." The cool tone in his voice was enough to turn the spa into an ice pond. "But I'm not putting my daughter on display, either. She can play in the home and for friends, and that's final."

"But you can't—"

"I said, that's final, Kat."

This was unbelievable! He wouldn't even discuss it. And the fact that he knew all along about Anna! Arms folded, Kat sank into the spa. Her insides felt as hot and swirling as the water she sat in. How could he be so stubborn, so close-minded, so...so pigheaded!

And as she realized why he was acting so obstinate, her irritation melted away.

He was afraid. Afraid that someone might hurt Anna, that they might take advantage of her, or use her. Or make fun of her. She was his little girl and he wanted to protect her, keep her safe. She couldn't fault him for that.

But she couldn't accept it, either. Not with a talent as brilliant as Anna's. Kat had no idea how she would ever change Logan's mind, but she knew she had to try. She thought briefly she might tell him who she was in order to give her argument credibility, but based on the hard set of his jaw and the hard look in his eyes, something told her that this wasn't the time. She'd let everything settle for the night and she'd tell him tomorrow.

He almost looked as if he'd fallen asleep. She'd never seen him so relaxed, and he had a boyish quality to him at the moment that made her want to take her fingers and comb back the hair falling onto his forehead.

She settled back in the hot water, trying to calm her jittery nerves. Just two adults, unwinding after a long day, nothing to be nervous about.

"I...I thought you had a date tonight," she said casually after a moment.

"I broke it."

"Oh." The sound of the rushing water became a roar in her ears. "Why?"

He opened his eyes and even in the shadowed moonlight, Kat could see the intensity under his dark lashes.

"You know why, Kat."

There was an earthy sensuality in his voice that she'd never heard before. Her heart skipped a beat. Did she? she wondered. Or had her fantasies taken control, and she no longer knew reality from illusion. She only knew what she wanted to believe, and she couldn't trust that, couldn't afford to make a mistake when she was so close to the edge.

"I need you to tell me," she said, her voice no more than a throaty whisper.

"Lord, woman," he said roughly, "does everything have to be difficult with you?"

"Tell me, Logan."

"What, that I want you? That I've thought about you every damn minute of every damn day since you got here?" His voice grew husky and deep. "Do you want me to tell you what those thoughts were, too? They might shock you, Kat. You might turn tail and run."

His words excited her. She stared at him, thankful she'd left the light off. The darkness gave her courage, a boldness she would normally not have dared.

"I won't run."

And then she noticed the pile of clothes lying a few feet from the spa and she almost did run.

Ohmygod…

He was naked. Beautifully and gloriously naked, not more than three feet away from her. Not that she could see anything other than his muscled shoulders and chest, but she knew it, and that realization made her body come alive.

"Come here, Kat."

She wanted to. God, how she wanted to. Still, she held back, her fear only heightening her excitement. Her heart pounded furiously against her chest.

"Logan, don't you think we should—"

"Yes, I do think we should. That's why I want you to come here."

And still she hesitated. She understood he wanted her to come to him so there'd be no doubt later that she'd given herself to him freely, that she wanted this as badly as he did.

And she did want it.

She felt his heated gaze on her. He waited, his face rigid, his body still. He hadn't offered a future, hadn't even implied that his need for her went beyond the physical. She was back to foolish daydreams and wild imaginings to think anything else. A man like Logan would never wait two years for her while she traveled the world and pursued her career. He was a man who needed to know that he and his daughter would be first priority in a woman's life.

There was no illusion here. This was reality. One night with Logan, a man she wanted more than any man. One night to discover each other, to put an end to the wondering that had plagued both of them. One night to remember, and cherish, the rest of her life.

She went to him.

He seemed to relax as she slowly closed the distance between them.

She stopped at an arm's length, careful not to touch him yet. His eyes were narrowed, and when his gaze dropped to the swell of her breasts, she felt herself tremble.

He said nothing, just stared at her, increasing her awareness of him. When he finally reached out, her breath caught. He fingered the thin strap of her bikini top and she waited, her pulse racing, for him to slip the strap off her shoulder.

But he didn't. Instead he slowly trailed his finger downward, following the line over the swell of her breasts. When his knuckles lightly brushed over the peaks of her hardened nipples, she closed her eyes and let out a soft sound of pleasure.

She felt the explosion of every tiny bubble against her breasts, her nipples, her stomach. And lower still. Like the water itself, her insides swirled hotly, its center the juncture of her legs.

He leaned closer and like a whisper, his mouth played over hers. Ever so softly, his warm, moist tongue tasted her bottom lip. She opened to him and met the gentle thrust of his tongue with her own. She felt weak and dizzy, and if not for the buoyancy of the water, her knees would have dissolved under her.

She placed her hands on his chest to steady herself and the contact was as powerful as touching an open circuit. He murmured something against her lips, then deepened the kiss, slanting his mouth against hers again and again.

When her hands moved over the hard planes of his chest, he drew in a sharp breath and pulled away.

"I wanted your hands on me since the first time I saw you," he said raggedly. "Almost as badly as I wanted mine on you."

He cupped her bottom with his hands, spreading his legs as he drew her to him and pulled her against him. She gasped at the press of his hardened arousal against her belly, shocked and excited at the same time.

She slid her arms around his neck, reveling in the feel of his powerful body against hers. His large hands kneaded her buttocks, then slid up her back and pressed her closer to him. She moved instinctively against him and he moaned, then caught her mouth again and kissed her fiercely.

His hands moved upward, over her thighs, her hips, her spine. She felt a quick flick of his fingers on the catch of her bikini top, and she pulled away, allowing the encumbering fabric to float away. Her breasts were tight and aching and when he cupped them in his hands, she bit her bottom lip to keep from crying out.

"You're so beautiful," he said, caressing the soft flesh. His thumbs slid back and forth over her nipples and she whimpered with the need that tore through her. He bent her backward, then closed his lips over one hardened peak. His tongue swirled over the sensitive tip and she buried her fingers in his thick hair, gasping at the intense pleasure that coursed through her.

He shifted his attention to her other breast, tasting her, teasing her until she thought she'd go crazy. Her fingers moved over his head and the sides of his face, wanting him closer still.

Steam swirled around their heads and shoulders, mixing with the cool night air, while the cascading water encased their lower bodies. Logan thought that he couldn't get enough of her. Every sound she made, every soft moan and whimper, drove him beyond the edge of control. He wanted, no *needed,* to touch her, to kiss her, everywhere at once. The fire building in him insisted that he hurry, that he possess her completely.

Reluctantly he left the sweet beauty of her breasts and cupped the back of her head with his hands. "I need you closer," he said roughly, then brought his mouth down on hers again. With her body pressed tightly to his, they both understood there was only one way for her to be any closer.

His hands slid over her shoulders, then under the water and down her sides. He slipped his fingers under the top of her bikini bottom and tugged the garment down. He felt her hesitate slightly and his first instinct was to drag her to him and plunge inside her before she could change her mind.

With a will of iron, he lifted his mouth from hers and looked into her face. Moonlight gleamed off her wet, flushed skin. Her eyelids, heavy with desire, opened slowly and she met his hard gaze.

"I want you more than I've ever wanted any woman," he said hoarsely. "But if you're not sure, Kat, if you have doubts, you have to tell me to stop now, right now. Five seconds from now, I don't know if I'll be able to."

Her breasts rose and fell with her labored breathing. Her lips, swollen from his kisses, parted, and her dark, passion-filled gaze dropped to his mouth. "Don't stop," she said softly. "Please don't stop."

Her brazen plea shocked Kat, but with Logan she felt powerful, as if she belonged here, as if she'd always belonged here. As he took her mouth again, the sound he made was low and guttural, and the knowledge that she had the ability to arouse him this way only increased her own excitement.

"I need to touch you." He slid his hands over her breasts, then down lower, over her belly, then lower still. The hot water swirled around them as he cupped her bottom. She felt suspended in air when he lifted her gently.

"Open your legs," he whispered, shifting his weight as he pulled her onto his lap.

Kat shivered at the need she heard in his voice and did

as he asked. She laid her hands on his upper arms, steadying herself, and felt the muscles in his arms tighten as his hands moved over her hips, then slid to the juncture of her legs. The texture of his work-roughened hands on the sensitive inside flesh of her thighs made her shudder. She made a soft, mewling sound and suddenly felt herself moving against him, needing him closer still.

Her encouragement brought a moan from deep inside Logan. She saw the grimace of pleasure-pain on his face. His hand moved over the most intimate part of her, caressing, stroking, and she thought she might fall apart at the intense sensation rippling through her.

"Logan," she gasped, moving against him. "Oh, Logan…"

"Kat," he said her name on a ragged breath. "Honey, I need you to stay right here…just like this…"

Confused, she opened her eyes slowly and saw him watching her with intensely dark eyes. "I'm not going anywhere."

He eased away from her. "I have to, just for a minute. I wasn't thinking before, I wanted you so badly. Until I get back, and I promise it won't be more than a minute, baby, I want you to just think about this—" he kissed her sensuously "—and this—" he slid his hand over her stomach "—and this." His hand slid lower and she shivered at the exquisite touch of his fingers on her body.

"Please hurry," she breathed.

He smiled. "No need to worry about that."

She lay back against the edge of the spa, letting her mind float with her body. The moon and darkness, the swirling water—even Logan—everything felt surreal to her. She wanted to savor the feeling, make it last forever. Her eyes drifted closed and every erotic burst of every bubble heightened her desire.

Good to his word, he was back in a minute. "Miss me?" he murmured as he pulled her to him.

"I almost sent out the search party." She nuzzled his neck, then slowly ran her fingers down his chest.

He laughed softly. "You keep your hand on that path and I guarantee you that you'll find me."

She did find him. His groan of pleasure brought a smile to her lips. She stroked the male hardness of him and felt a sense of power she'd never experienced before. She finally understood what it felt like to truly be a woman, and the realization thrilled her, excited her beyond anything she'd ever known.

She continued to explore his body, reveling in her newfound freedom. His legs were long and powerful, the muscles on his stomach, chest and arms like sculpted iron. His body was magnificent. He watched her through hooded eyes, his gaze fierce and primitive.

And then he touched her. Gently. His thumbs brushed her hardened nipples, then his hands cupped her breasts and lightly squeezed. He moved lower and caressed the sensitive flesh between her legs. She moaned, clutching his shoulders as she moved against him. And when his finger slid inside her, she gasped. He stroked her, bringing her fever to a wild pitch.

She couldn't stand any more. She needed him desperately, fully. She rose over him, lifting herself partially out of the water, exposing her bare breasts to him while she positioned her body over his. He took her breasts in his hands and closed his lips over one nipple, pulling, tugging, bringing her beyond recognition of time or place.

She lowered herself, hesitating at the first resistance, then slowly, very slowly, easing herself onto the smooth steel strength of him. His fingers closed around her hips and tightened almost painfully, guiding her closer. Deeper.

"Kat..." he groaned her name over and over, and as she began to move, he sucked in his breath. He grew bigger inside her, harder, and she bit her lip, struggling to contain the last tiny vestige of control.

How could she have ever known it would be like this? That she could lose so much more to him than her body? She knew, without a doubt, as certain as the sun rose, that no other man could ever bring her to this, that she would never want another man to even try.

He filled her with more than his body, and that knowledge brought tears to her eyes. She brought her mouth to his, kissed him fiercely, praying she might tell him with her body what her lips could not. His tongue met hers roughly, urgently, and she wrapped her arms tightly around his neck. He thrust gently upward, setting a primitive rhythm that Kat followed. The rhythm increased and she clung to him as the heat inside them coiled tighter and tighter.

Pleasure became torture, an exquisite pain that demanded release. And as the water churned and raged around her body, that release came in a shower of white-hot explosions. Kat cried out, digging her fingers into his arms and rolling her head against his shoulder. Logan nearly crushed her to him as he thrust deeply into her, then shuddered convulsively with a deep guttural moan.

It was impossible to move so she lay still, with her head on his shoulder, waiting for her heart to slow and her breathing to subside. With a long, heavy release of breath, Logan loosened his tight hold on her and cradled her in his arms, kissing her temple and ear.

She waited for the guilt to come, the regret. There was none. Just blissful contentment and acceptance of the moment, an understanding that neither one of them could have prevented this, not only because they both wanted it, but because it was meant to be.

Sighing softly, she pressed her lips to his damp neck. "Looks like I didn't miss the fireworks, after all," she whispered with a smile.

Propped up against his headboard, with Kat nestled snugly in his arms, Logan found himself grinning.

Before tonight, after he'd made love with a woman, including his ex-wife, he'd always felt a strange need to distance himself, to close himself off. He'd accepted that as a part of himself, as a flaw or defect in his character. An inability to truly connect intimately with a woman.

But not with Kat.

After they'd made love, he'd wrapped her in a towel and carried her into his bedroom, feeling as if that was where she'd belonged all along. In his bed, with him. When he'd left her for a moment and gone in search of his terry-cloth robe, he felt as if he'd been gone two hours instead of two minutes.

And now, with her lying across his chest, with her wet hair a tumbled mass of dark curls and her skin still flushed from the spa and their lovemaking, he wanted her closer still.

"You hungry?" He brushed her hair away from her cheek.

She laughed softly and rose up to look at him. "Men. Satisfy one need and they move to another."

He widened his grin. "Who said I was satisfied?"

She gasped as he flipped her onto her back then tangled her fingers in his hair as he kissed her neck.

"You're a greedy man, Logan Kincaid," she murmured, arching her neck to give him more room to explore.

"Very greedy," he muttered, tugging open the V of her robe and trailing hot kisses over her shoulder and down to her breasts. She clutched him to her and moaned.

He pushed the robe out of his way as he moved lower still, tasting the soft valleys and delicate angles of her body. When he moved lower still, to the petal soft curve of her thighs, she drew in a sharp breath and stiffened.

"Logan," she breathed, "I don't know, I mean, I've never…"

"Shh," he tenderly caressed her hips and slid his hands underneath her. "Just relax, sweetheart, let me love you."

Slowly, as he moved over her, she did relax, then her body tightened again, this time with passion. Her hands moved restlessly, her body arched and writhed under him. She called his name, muttered a few words he was surprised she knew, and when she fell over the edge, gasping, he felt more satisfied himself than he could have ever imagined.

She lay there, her breathing heavy, and he wanted to cover her body with his, to consume her. But he held himself back, wanting to savor this moment as hers alone. He felt a strong sense of male pride, knowing that he'd left a mark, that he'd given her something she'd never had before.

"Now who's greedy?" he whispered, sliding his body up alongside hers.

Her cheeks flushed bright red. "I always wondered about that," she said breathlessly.

He laughed softly at her honest, guileless statement. He'd never met a woman like her before, hadn't believed one existed. No pretensions, no games. She spoke from her heart.

He pulled her close to him, listening to the beat of her heart, wondering what it spoke to her now. About him. He hadn't the courage to ask, everything he was feeling himself was too new to him. He needed time to understand what was happening between them, *if* something was happening between them.

Her breathing grew even and steady and he cradled her in his arms, then gave in to his own exhaustion and closed his eyes.

A bright light woke him. He blinked several times, then sat, disoriented. The bed beside him was empty and he felt a stab of disappointment. He'd wanted to wake up with her next to him, naked and tousled.

"Time to get up, lazy bones."

At the sound of Kat's voice, he turned and saw her standing in front of the sliding glass door where she'd just opened the drapes. She smiled at him, then opened the slider, letting in the cool morning air.

His disappointment deepened as he realized she'd dressed already, but when the light passed through the thin cotton sundress she wore, silhouetting her body, and the breeze lifted the hem of her skirt, he decided that was a pretty great way to wake up, also.

"Yeah," he said, his voice rough, "why don't you come here and say that to my face. I'll show you lazy."

"It's late," she said with all the proper diction of a schoolteacher. "You have to get up."

"I am up," he said with an evil grin, catching hold of her arm and pulling her into bed with him. "And it's not that late."

She laughed as he covered her mouth with his, then slid her arms around his neck and met the deep thrust of his tongue with her own. Her skin felt cool and silky against his and he laid her back, tugging the sheet out of his way so he could pull her under him.

But she was too quick. She bounced out of bed again, bringing the sheet with her. "Anna's going to be home soon."

He sighed and dragged a hand through his hair. He was definitely not in the mood for talk right now. He looked at her, saw the passion flare in her green eyes as she met his gaze. He stood and started for her.

"Oh, no, you don't," she gasped and backed away from him toward the door. "I have coffee in the kitchen and I'll make us something to eat while you get dressed."

She dropped the sheet and ran out the door as he took another step toward her. Frowning, he grabbed the sheet then cursed himself for sleeping so late. His crew was already out on the ranch, and he knew he should just get dressed and join them.

He heard Kat in the kitchen, humming, and smiled. Maybe he would have breakfast. He was the boss, wasn't he? He didn't have to explain himself to anyone if he showed up a little late.

A few minutes later he followed the smell of bacon and pancakes in the kitchen. She stood at the griddle and he moved behind her, slipping his arms around her waist and pulling her against him.

She leaned back, pressing her body into his. He kissed

her neck and moved his hands upward to her breasts. She shivered, then moved abruptly away from him and grabbed a plate of pancakes.

"Logan, we need to talk." She moved to the kitchen table and sat.

With a sigh, he sat across from her and took her hand. "Look, Kat, if you're going to tell me that we shouldn't have made love last night, then I don't want to—"

"Last night was wonderful," she said softly.

Relief poured through Logan. He turned her hand over in his, marveling at the smooth texture of her silky skin and long, slender fingers.

But if she didn't want to talk about last night, then what? She looked much too serious to be discussing the evening meal or one of Anna's lessons.

Anna. That's what she wanted to talk about. He recognized that determined lift of her chin.

He let loose of her hand and sat back in his chair. "I told you. My daughter is not going to be anybody's entertainment. She does not, and will not, perform publicly."

Kat had just prepared herself to tell Logan who she really was and now he was talking about Anna. She paused, uncertain which way to take the conversation, then decided since he'd brought it up, she'd better take advantage of the opportunity to discuss Anna.

"Logan." She touched his arm. "A talent like Anna's is rare. Very rare. It's a gift that needs to be nurtured. She needs schooling and—"

"Don't tell me what my daughter needs." He looked at her and his eyes were like blue ice. "What she needs is to be with people who love her, not people who will exploit her and use her for their own benefit."

"It's not like that." Kat forced her voice to be calm. "Anna has a special gift, the chance for a brilliant future."

"What the hell future is there for her," he said angrily, "to build up her hopes, then see her rejected or dismissed at the whim of some idiot who would only remember her as a girl in a wheelchair who played a fair fiddle?"

Kat shook her head, determined to make him understand. "Anna is a prodigy, Logan. She's already way beyond what the most accomplished musician could ever hope for. The possibilities for her are endless."

"Possibilities?" The chair scraped across the floor as he pushed away from the table. "Like yours? Looking for work between gigs, or whatever the hell you call what you do?"

She flinched at his words, but realized it was time. Time to tell him the truth about herself. "Logan—"

The sound of car horns honking stopped her. Swearing, Logan strode stiffly past her to the front door, but before he reached it, Tom walked in, wheeling an excited Anna.

"Daddy!" she cried. "Reporters are here and TV cameras and all kinds of people."

"What the hell—" Logan looked out the front window.

"One of the reporters said something about a famous violinist," Tom said.

"Dammit!" Eyes narrowed, Logan turned to Kat. "I told you this would happen. One little performance and suddenly there's media crawling all over my house."

Fists clenched, he moved for the front door.

"Logan!" Kat stepped in front of him. "What are you going to do?"

"I'm going to tell them to get the hell out of here," he said furiously. "They aren't talking to my daughter."

He tried to move around her, but she took hold of his arm and held him back. "Logan, no, listen to me, they aren't here to talk to Anna."

He looked down at her. "What are you talking about?"

"They aren't here for Anna," she repeated, her voice shaking.

Confusion darkened his eyes. "Then who are they here for?"

She drew in a deep breath and met his hard gaze.

"Me." She let her hand drop from his arm. "They're here for me."

Nine

Katrina Natalya Delaney.

Logan stood at the window in his office and stared blankly out at the corral. Tom was exercising a horse while Anna watched from under a nearby oak tree.

Katrina Natalya Delaney.

World-famous violinist virtuoso. Daughter of the illustrious Delaney Designs, one of New York's most celebrated fashion moguls.

He racked his brain trying to remember why it all sounded vaguely familiar. *Forbes*. That was it. He'd read an article in the magazine several months ago about the Delaneys, but the piece had been about the father and mother.

Turning sharply, he moved to the bookcase behind his desk and dug through the stack of magazines until he found the one he was looking for.

Page fifty-four. Delaney Designs:, the title read, A Pattern For Success.

A picture of Larisa and Nicolai Delaney covered the first

page. Larisa's shining dark hair, soft smile and deep green eyes gave her an ageless beauty, while Nicolai's salt-and-pepper temples, gray eyes and square jaw emanated strength and power. He skimmed the article.

...Russian immigrants...factory worker and seamstress...hardworking...started own company in basement...

Kat—he clenched his teeth—*Katrina* had told him all that, though she'd certainly mitigated the magnitude of her parents' company.

And her own exceptional career.

Eyes narrowed, he turned the page and there she was, standing between her parents at a children's benefit where she'd performed. She wore a gold sequined dress her mother had designed for her, a formfitting, low-cut gown that would have any man running into walls. She was every bit the picture of sophistication and elegance.

He knew what she felt like under that dress, what she tasted like, but he had no idea who the woman herself was.

He read on. The article discussed her upcoming two-year world tour and linked her with Brad Pitt, Richard Gere and a cellist named Oliver Grant.

Oliver? The same one she'd called frequently, no doubt. With a curse, he crumpled the magazine and threw it across his office. He heard the knock at the door and ignored it, then ignored it the second time, too.

"Logan?" She opened the door slowly and stepped into the room. "Can I come in?"

"Looks like you have," he said flatly.

The torn magazine lay at Kat's feet. She bent to pick it up and her fingers shook as she smoothed the pages then laid it on his desk.

"I'm sorry about the reporters," she said quietly. "I got rid of them as quickly as I could, but they wanted a few pictures and a statement." She sighed heavily. "I found out that Trudy Goodhouse called them. It never occurred to me that if she recognized me she might call the newspapers."

"It obviously never occurred to you that anyone would

recognize you," he said sarcastically. "But then, who, in a podunk town like Harmony would ever recognize an acclaimed violin virtuoso hiding out from her adoring fans in New York?"

"I'm not hiding out," she said quickly. "At least, not like you think."

"You wouldn't want to know what I think, Kat. Oh, excuse me, I mean *Katrina*."

Kat felt her insides twist at the icy politeness in Logan's voice. She knew he'd be upset, knew that he had a right to be, but still she hated the mocking tone in his words. "I never lied to you. I told you why I came here and it's the truth. I've always loved the West. I wanted to experience—"

"Ah, yes. Experience. Your chance to live your fantasies." One corner of his mouth lifted in a sardonic grin. "So tell me, *Katrina*, since I was obviously part of your little game, too, was jumping into bed with a cowboy everything you'd thought it would be? I'd hate to think I disappointed you."

She felt the blood drain from her face, then very carefully met his cool gaze. "Don't do that, Logan," she whispered. "Don't turn the most wonderful night of my life into something dirty."

A muscle twitched in his jaw as he stared at her. "You never struck me as a one-night girl, Kat. Is that how it was with Brad and Richard and Oliver?"

A coldness settled inside her at Logan's cruel remark. She'd always been a patient person, but there were limits to that patience, and she'd reached hers.

"I don't deserve that, Logan," she said softly, then turned and headed for the door. "I'll be out of here by the evening."

She was opening the door when he reached from behind her and slammed it closed again. With a gasp, she turned, her back to the door. He towered over her, his face rigid and his eyes angry.

"Running away again?" He placed one arm on either side of her.

He was eight inches taller than her and outweighed her by a hundred pounds, but she refused to be intimidated or bullied by him. What she couldn't stop, what she hated herself for, was the shiver of excitement that coursed through her at his closeness. "I don't normally stay where I'm not wanted."

"Oh, you're wanted all right," he said heavily and her heart began to race. "Just not by me. It's Anna who will be most hurt if you leave and I'll do anything to keep that hurt away from her. Even tolerate you being around for the next month."

In spite of the pain his words caused, she realized he wanted her to stay. For Anna, of course, but still, he was, in his own way, asking her to stay.

But could she? Could she be in the same house with him, share meals and polite conversation, then go to her bedroom every night, knowing he was so close and wanted nothing to do with her?

Yes, she thought, lifting her chin. For Anna, she could. And she realized at that moment that she loved the child, truly loved her, and would do anything for her, even stay here, though it would mean a torment beyond anything she'd ever known.

Because she also realized with ironic clarity, that she loved Logan, too.

And that was something she would never let him know.

Drawing from a strength she didn't know she possessed, she squared her shoulders and leveled her gaze with his. "All right," she said stiffly. "For Anna, I'll stay. And that's the only reason."

His mouth was a hard, firm line. He eased away from her and she held her back straight as she left the room, waiting until she got to her room before she allowed her legs to crumple under her.

* * *

"Katrina, darling, please, end this foolishness and come home."

Kat rolled her eyes and shifted the phone to her other ear. "Mom, I told you. I'll be home in three weeks."

It was the same conversation they'd had every day for the past week, since the entertainment newspapers and tabloids had gotten hold of the story that Katrina Natalya Delaney had taken a job as a nanny on a cattle ranch in Texas. Her mother would plead with her to come home, then put her father on the phone.

"But Katrina, the stories we hear in the papers! Sydney Joyce wrote that you were having a wild love affair, and *Music Today* said that you were recovering from an accident and you'll never play again. Max nearly had a heart attack over that one."

Exasperated, Kat shook her head at the absurdity. "I only wish the first were true," she said, then laughed when her mother gasped. "As for the second, tell poor Max he hasn't lost a client, yet."

"Your father and I are worried sick about you," her mother went on. "Here, talk to your father."

With a heavy sigh, Kat waited until her father was on the line.

"Katrina, this is ridiculous. You're upsetting your mother. Come home at once."

"Dad," she said patiently, "you don't have to worry about me. I'm fine, perfectly fine."

That was a lie. She was miserable. Logan had avoided her for the past week as if she were the plague. He worked longer hours, leaving at sunrise and sometimes not getting home until long after dark. He ate breakfast and lunch with his crew out on the range, and though he still ate dinner with them, the conversation was a strained politeness.

He was a stubborn, bullheaded man and she loved him so much her heart ached. But the things he'd said to her still echoed in her mind: *you wouldn't want to know what I think…was jumping into bed with a cowboy everything you'd thought it would be…is that how it was with Brad and Richard and Oliver?* The pain of those words cut through her. She felt open and raw. Defeated.

The only bright spot had been Anna. She was the only reason Kat stayed. Anna was excited about studying with a real-life violinist. She eagerly looked forward to her music lessons, but when it came to her other studies, or even her riding lessons with her father, she seemed quieter. She wasn't eating as well, and she'd even turned down an invitation to spend the weekend at Julie's. It had taken a lot of encouragement to get her to change her mind, but Anna had finally agreed and had seemed to brighten when they'd been packing a bag for her a little while ago.

And when Kat realized that she and Logan were going to be alone again, for the weekend, she'd made a few plans of her own.

"Katrina! Do you hear me? Are you there?"

She suddenly realized her father had been speaking to her. "Yes, Dad, I'm here. But I have to go now. Give my love to Mom."

After a few more appeals for her return home, Kat hung up the phone, then closed her eyes and leaned back against the kitchen counter with a heavy sigh.

"Where are you going?"

Startled, she opened her eyes. Logan stood at the back door, staring at her overnight bag she'd set on the table with her purse and sweater. She wondered how long he'd been standing there, then decided it didn't matter.

His gaze skimmed over her, assessing her short, off-the-shoulder black knit dress. She'd also applied makeup and put on her pearl-drop earrings. After a week of masculine rejection, she'd felt the need to put on something pretty. On impulse, she'd even dared a spray of her mother's new perfume, *Siren.* She watched Logan's eyes narrow to dark slits as he stared at her.

"I'm going into town for the weekend," she said casually. "Since Anna isn't going to be here, I thought I'd take a couple of days off."

He looked at her, and she saw his jaw muscle work back and forth. "How are you getting there?"

Intentionally avoiding eye contact with Logan, Kat walked over to the table and pulled on her black sweater. "Tom's giving me a lift in when he's done working. Sophia's going to stay with Anna until Julie's mom picks her up in a little while. There's a casserole in the refrigerator you can warm up if you're hungry and Julie's phone number is on the notepad by the bread box."

Her voice was detached and indifferent, but her insides were shaking. Why had he come home early? And today, of all days!

To say goodbye to Anna, she realized. He knew that his daughter was going to Julie's and he would want to see her before she left. *Damn!* Why hadn't she considered that?

Logan still hadn't moved. He just stood stiffly at the doorway, watching her. "Why didn't you ask for the car? You have a license now, you could drive yourself."

She fiddled with the contents of her purse, arranging and rearranging, wishing to God that Tom would hurry. "It wasn't necessary, thank you."

"How are you getting home?" he asked tightly.

She snapped her purse closed and turned to meet his hard gaze. "I don't see how that's any concern of yours."

A muscle twitched under his right eye. "Dammit, Kat, you can't just go—"

A knock at the back door cut him off. Kat breathed a sigh of relief. She hadn't been prepared for another confrontation with Logan. She was too vulnerable right now, her emotions too exposed.

"Yes, Logan, I can just go," she said quietly, then picked up her purse and weekend bag and brushed past him.

Logan watched her walk past him with the air of a grand duchess. He'd never seen this haughty side of her and he sure as hell didn't like it. He struggled between dragging her back and putting his fist through the wall. When she walked out the back door, he swore and kicked the plastic wastebasket beside the refrigerator. It flew, slamming into the wall across the room. At least the damn thing was empty, he thought irritably.

What did he care where she went? he thought, yanking his hat off his head and throwing it. She could go anywhere she damn well pleased.

He began to pace. Was she spending the weekend with Tom? No, he didn't think so. Tom was seeing a girl in Southcreek. At least, he *had* been seeing her. Logan had never paid much attention to his crew's love lives. It wasn't his business what his employees did on their off hours.

Kat was his employee, too, he realized. What she did wasn't his business, either.

Frowning, he kicked the kitchen chair. Damn, but she'd looked beautiful. She'd taken his breath away when he'd walked in and seen her in that slinky little dress. She'd combed her hair different, too, sort of half piled those dark shining tresses on top of her head and let a few silky curls tumble around her neck.

And her smell. A perfume she hadn't worn before. A perfume that begged a man to come closer. It had taken every ounce of willpower not to drag her into his bedroom, peel that dress off her and plunge his body into hers. That's what he'd wanted to do.

That's what he still wanted to do.

She'd done this intentionally, he decided, gritting his teeth. She'd known this would torture him, that he'd be home, wondering where she was and who she was with. That was part of her game, too. To make him wild for her, out of his head.

It was working.

He stopped, closing his eyes as he caught the scent she'd left behind. He dragged it into his lungs and held it there. He *was* crazy for her. Not a minute had passed since he'd found out she'd lied to him that he hadn't wanted her. Not a night had passed that he hadn't walked to his bedroom door, cursed himself, and her, then walked the floor. He'd done his best to avoid her, worked his butt off so he'd be too tired to think about her. It hadn't worked. Nothing had worked.

She'd gotten into his blood. More deeply, more strongly than any other woman ever had.

Damn it to hell!

He kicked the kitchen chair again, upsetting it. She was leaving in three weeks. She had her career. Her world tour. She had Brad and Richard and Oliver.

He went still, remembering what he'd said to her about being a one-night stand and that she'd slept with all those men. It made him sick to think he'd said that to her. He knew it wasn't true. She might not have been a virgin, but she was pretty damn close. There had been an innocence about her that was Kat's alone. Sweet and pure and refreshing.

With a heavy sigh, he righted the chair and scooted it under the table. He wouldn't think about her. He wouldn't. He'd go insane if he did.

"Daddy?"

He turned sharply. Anna sat in her wheelchair at the doorway to the kitchen, watching him, her brow furrowed.

"What, sweetheart?" He moved beside her and knelt down.

"Are you mad at Kat?" she asked quietly.

"No," he said truthfully. He was mad at himself now.

"Are you mad at me?"

"Of course not. Why would I be mad at you?"

"Because I played the violin at the festival."

He hadn't realized that Anna had sensed his disapproval. He'd never said anything to her about it. "It's all right, Anna. You were wonderful."

"I won't play anymore." He saw the tears in her eyes. "I'll be good and do all my lessons, but please don't be mad at me and please don't make Kat go away."

It felt as if someone had reached inside his chest and ripped out his heart. He swallowed hard, then cleared his throat. "Anna, Kat only went to town. She'll be back Sunday. And I'm not mad at you, I promise. If you want to play the violin, you can."

She smiled slowly. "I can?"

He wiped a tear off her cheek with his thumb. "We'll find a teacher for you and start lessons whenever you want."

"Kat will give me lessons. She's what's called a virtuoso. She says I can be one, too."

"Sweetheart, you know Kat can't stay here forever. She has to leave in three weeks."

"You could ask her to stay. She likes us, doesn't she?"

She likes *you*, Logan thought. *Me she'd just as soon wrap in barbed wire and push over a cliff.* "She can't stay, Anna. She has a job to do. A lot of people need her."

"I need her," Anna whispered.

The front doorbell rang. Logan gave his daughter a hug. "We'll talk about this when you come back, sweetheart. Just go and have a good time at Julie's."

And after Logan got Anna off and Sophia left and the house was silent again, he sat at the kitchen table, smelled the lingering scent of Kat's perfume and finally admitted to himself that he needed her, too.

The Longhorn Bar and Grill was where it was happening on Friday nights in Harmony. A country and western band called *Untamed* played the top hits while steaks sizzled on an open grill in the back of the room. Because the music was loud and the food good, the bar and restaurant drew a large crowd from not only the people of Harmony, but from the neighboring towns, as well.

Amidst all the noise and smoke, Kat sat in a booth with Tom and his girlfriend, Debbie, drinking a beer and nibbling on taco chips and salsa. Debbie, a fun-loving pretty redhead who worked as a hairdresser, was telling a story about one of her male customers.

"So he brings me this brown bag," Debbie said, and started to giggle, "and here's this piece of ratty fur inside. He calls it his unit."

"Calls what his unit?" Kat asked.

"You know, his rug, his hairpiece. He calls it his unit."

Kat couldn't help but smile at the image of a grown man calling a toupee his "unit."

"Bartender—" Debbie stopped short in the middle of her story to wave to a cute little blonde "—we need some tequila shooters here, *por favor.*"

"So anyway," Debbie went on, struggling to maintain her composure, "he leaves and tells me he'll be back in an hour or two. I have another customer I'm working on and after I'm done I'm gonna do the 'unit,' only the bag is gone."

Kat nearly choked in the middle of taking a drink of beer. "I'm afraid to ask."

Debbie was laughing hard now. "One of the other customers, a little old lady who doesn't see well, always brings her lunch to the salon when we do a perm. She hadn't finished her banana and it was still in the bag, so she took it. Only she took the wrong one."

Tom was grinning, too, shaking his head in disbelief as he swigged his beer.

"I declare," Debbie said between gasps of air, "I think we could have heard her scream all the way from San Antonio. She threw it, and her dog, Mitzi, took off under the bed with it. By the time I got there, Mitzi thought that unit was a new friend and didn't want to part with it. We played tug-of-war for fifteen minutes."

They were all laughing now. Tears streamed down Debbie's face.

"Who won?" Tom asked.

"We both did!" Debbie screamed, then burst into hysterics again.

Tom and Kat were still laughing after Debbie ran off to fix her makeup. The waitress set the shooters down, smiled at Tom, then sashayed away.

Kat stared at the shot glass, wedge of lime and saltshaker. She rarely drank, and she'd never had tequila. "I have no idea what to do with this," she admitted.

"Well, every day's a brand-new experience," Tom said. "Watch me."

He made a fist and licked the back of his hand just above his thumb, sprinkled salt there, licked it again, then downed the tequila and sucked on the lime. Eyes wide, Kat stared at him.

"You expect me to do that?" she gasped.

"Life's too short not to try new things," Tom took a long pull on his beer.

Why not? she thought. He was right. Life was too short. And right now, life was miserable, too. If she could forget about Logan for just a few minutes, then the headache tomorrow would be worth it.

She did exactly as Tom had done. Made the fist, licked, salted, licked, then threw back the tequila. It burned all the way down and she choked. She was reaching for the lime when a shadow fell over the table.

"Mind if I join you?"

Logan.

Her heart stopped, then started to race. He sat beside her without waiting for an answer.

"Hi, Tom." There was no smile on Logan's mouth as he stared at his foreman.

"Uh, hi, Logan." When Logan said nothing else, Tom shifted uncomfortably and pulled his hat low on his head. "I, uh, better go look for Debbie."

After Tom slid out of the booth, Logan turned back to Kat. "You forgot the lime," he said, handing her the slice of fruit.

She forced her hands to be still as she took the lime from him, but when her fingers brushed his, she felt a ripple of electricity go through her. Holding his gaze, she put the slice of citrus to her mouth and sucked the sour juice. Logan's eyes darkened as he watched her and when she put the beer bottle to her lips and took a swallow, as she'd seen Tom do, she could have sworn she heard a growl deep in Logan's chest.

And then it was her turn to watch him.

Her breath caught as he went through the same motions she had. His tongue dampened his hand, he salted and licked it, threw back the tequila, then reached for the lime. She wanted to look away, to ignore him even, but she might as well have told a river to flow upstream. His lips were damp from the tequila and lime and she knew what he'd taste like right now. Tangy and warm. Salty.

No. She wasn't going to let him sweep her away like this. She wasn't. But when he reached across her and she watched him take a drink of her beer, there was no denying where she wanted his lips. On her mouth. On her face, her neck, her breasts.

She dragged her gaze from his and stared at the glass candle dome on the table. "What are you doing here, Logan?" she asked quietly.

He shrugged. "I like the music here."

"From this particular booth?"

"Especially from this booth."

She sighed. She was trapped on the inside of the booth and was already as far over to the wall as she could get. "Logan, if you don't mind, I'm waiting for someone."

He raised one eyebrow, then waved the waitress for another beer. "Who?"

"What business is that of yours?"

"Who?"

She folded her arms and sat straight against the back of the booth. "Brad," she said, then tapped her cheek with her finger. "Or was it Richard? No, wait a minute, it was Oliver. I just can't keep them straight."

He sighed. "Okay, I deserved that."

"Yes, you did."

He tipped his black Stetson back, then got up out of the booth and started to walk away. Her heart sank.

He turned suddenly and walked back.

"How do, ma'am." He touched the brim of his hat. "My name's Logan Kincaid. Haven't I seen you here before?"

What in the world was he doing? "Logan, sit down," she hissed. "People are looking."

"Why thank you, ma'am, I'd love to sit." He scooted into the booth across from her. "Can I buy you a drink? Did anyone ever tell you that you have beautiful eyes?"

He was using every bad come-on line that the masculine gender had ever created. And loudly. She glanced around at the people staring and sank into her seat. "Will you lower your voice?"

"That sure is a pretty dress you're wearing," he drawled heavily. "And you smell nicer than a bouquet of pink daisies."

In spite of herself, she laughed at his silly compliment.

He tugged on the brim of his hat and frowned. "You're not supposed to laugh when I'm trying to pick you up."

Pick her up? Is that what he was doing? She warmed at the thought, but refused to take his absurd behavior seriously. "Logan Kincaid," she said, shaking her head as she laughed, "you're a crazy man."

"That I am," he said with a grin, but there was an intensity in his eyes that made her pulse skip.

He reached across the table then and took her hand. "I never should have said what I did to you," he said quietly. "But I felt as if you'd lied to me and Anna, used us even, and—"

"I'd never—"

"Be quiet," he said firmly. "It's damn hard enough apologizing without having to start over."

Apologizing? Is that what Logan was doing? Stunned, all Kat could do was stare.

"I know you aren't like that. I was angry. And when I'm mad I haven't got a lick of good sense. All I could do was react. I've had your proverbial bee on my butt all week, and tonight, when I saw you were going out, that bee gave me a good sting. I knew that any man who looked at you would want you as bad as I do." He rubbed his thumb over hers. "It made me crazy to think that you might be with someone else."

Despite the delicious tingles running up her spine at Logan's touch, she pulled her hand away. "In spite of what you think of me, Logan, I don't sleep around."

"I know that, Kat, I told you, I was just—"

"Now you let *me* finish," she demanded, blushing furiously. "I've only been with one man before. He was an instructor in college. It was brief, and it was definitely a mistake."

"You don't have to tell me this, it doesn't—"

"Yes, I do have to tell you this. Because I think that whether you admit it or not, you are always going to wonder about whatever the newspapers or tabloids might print about me. For the record, I shook hands and said hello to Richard and Brad once, and Oliver is just a friend. Any future stories you hear or read about you'll have to decide for yourself."

His face hardened at her words, then he leaned over the table and stuck his jaw out. "How 'bout you just hit me, honey. Lord knows, putting up with me, you earned it. We'll both feel better."

She could think of other things that would make them both feel better, but she thought she might shock him if she told him what they were. She just shook her head instead. "You are crazy," she said with a laugh.

He grinned at her as the band switched from a line-dance to a fast two-step. He grabbed her hand suddenly and dragged her with him out of the booth and onto the dance floor. Slipping one arm around her waist, he pulled her close and moved around the floor. Her head spun as she struggled to keep up with him.

And then the band did an about-face again and began to play a sensual slow song. She was still in Logan's arms, but he hadn't moved, he just stared at her, his smile fading and his eyes darkening. Slowly he pulled her against him and held her close as he began to move. His body was hard and strong and she felt the heat of his skin through the navy blue Western shirt he wore. She caught the masculine scent of his aftershave and the smell of lime. The feel of his warm breath on her neck made her heart pound low and heavy in her chest.

Around them, the other couples came together on the dance floor, their arms wrapped around each other as they swayed to the music. Music brought people together, she knew. It made them feel, if only for a few minutes, that the outside world didn't matter.

But when the song ended, when the lead singer in the band stepped to the microphone and called out her name, she knew that reality had stepped back in, and there was no denying, or running away from, the outside world.

"...and if y'all didn't know, we have a national celebrity with us here tonight—" the singer looked at Katrina and everyone turned toward her "—so everybody clap your hands and give a big cheer and if we're lucky, Miss Katrina might honor us with a tune."

She felt Logan stiffen beside her, and when his hand fell away from her waist, she felt cold and empty.

Everyone watched her, including Logan, waiting for her. Torn, she looked at the band, then back to Logan. His face was rigid, but he said nothing. She didn't want to do this. She didn't. She wanted desperately to be two people: one to be the Katrina who played the violin, one to be the Katrina who loved Logan Kincaid.

But she couldn't have it all. Not with Logan. To think that she could was as dangerous as it was foolish.

Because she *was* Katrina Natalya Delaney. She could not give up who she was for anyone. Not even for Logan.

The crowd parted and amongst the applause she moved stiffly to the stage, a smile on her lips she didn't feel. She conferred briefly with the band, choosing a well-known piece about doing battle with the devil. Considering her situation with Logan, the number seemed only fitting.

But as she played, as she slipped into what had always come naturally to her, what had always made her feel alive, she lost herself to the passion. There was no crowd, no smoke-filled restaurant, no waiters or waitresses clinking glasses or serving drinks.

And when she finished her piece, as the crowd cheered and whistled, she also realized there was no Logan.

Ten

Logan stood in the parking lot outside the restaurant, one hand on the open door of his pickup and the other hand digging for the keys in his pocket. He could still hear the muffled music and an occasional outburst of laughter from the crowd inside, but out here the night was cool and clear and quiet.

Frustration tore at his gut. His temper was frayed. A tension built inside him that was almost unbearable.

He slammed the pickup door closed and leaned against the truck's bed with a heavy sigh.

He shouldn't have left. He knew that. But there seemed to be a lack of communication with himself between what he *should* have done and what he *had* done.

He took off his hat and turned it around and around in his hands. It was a blow to his pride to admit it, but he was a coward. A low-life, yellow-bellied, snake-crawling coward.

"Damn you, Logan Kincaid."

Startled, Logan looked up. Kat. He hadn't heard her

come up, but she stood a few away, her eyes narrowed and lips pressed tightly together. "Kat—"

She didn't give him a chance to say any more. She turned abruptly and walked away, arms stiffly at her sides and head straight.

Cursing under his breath, he followed her. "Kat, look," he said tersely, "I can't—"

She ignored him and kept walking, past the restaurant, then across the street.

"Will you just stop for a minute and—"

She walked past Stubbs's diner and started for the motel.

Apologies had never been easy, and he'd already used up his yearly quota earlier when he'd said he was sorry. He wasn't a man to explain himself, and he sure as hell wasn't going to apologize again.

She had the motel room key in her hand. Two seconds and she'd be to the door and inside. He reached out and took hold of her arm and turned her around.

Tears streamed down her cheeks. Her eyes were red and her cheeks flushed.

Son of a bitch.

His own anger and frustration dissipated and he cursed himself again. That's what he was. A son of a bitch.

"Kat," he said softly, pulling her to him, "I'm sorry I left like I did. I shouldn't have."

She resisted him, folding her arms across her chest in a protective gesture. He held her firmly, trying to get her to look at him, but she turned her head away.

"I don't know what happened to me," he said. "There you were on the stage, everyone cheering and looking at you and something just snapped. I had to get out of there or I swear I would have dragged you off that stage and out of the restaurant."

She said nothing, but at least she was looking at him now.

"Don't you understand?" he said, his voice gravelly. "Don't you know that I don't want to share you with anyone? That I want you to belong to me and nobody else?"

There. He'd said it. He hadn't completely realized it himself until this second. She blinked several times and he felt her relax in his arms.

"When I realized that I can't have you to myself," he said quietly, "that I'd have to share you, that I'd always have to share you, I felt crazy. I had to get out of there."

The night breeze caught the loose curls around Kat's face. She slowly released the breath she'd been holding.

"This is who I am," Kat whispered. "Who I'll always be. I wish I could tell you that I'm sorry I misled you, but if you had known who I was, you never would have let me be Anna's nanny. I never would have been a part of her life, or her a part of mine." Her moisture-filled eyes softened as she met his gaze. "And I'd never have known you, either. Logan Kincaid would never have been a part of my life, and I never would have been part of his. And for that I'll never be sorry."

He listened to her words, stunned, and at the same time, touched by them. Did he feel the same way? Was he glad that she'd come into his and Anna's life, knowing that he'd have to let her go, that she would never truly belong to them? There'd been little pain for himself when JoAnn had left, it was Anna he had hurt for. But Kat...

It felt as if a steel band were squeezing his chest. He pulled her tighter, almost roughly against him, and breathed in the scent of her. He moved his lips over her temple and against her hair. She sighed and relaxed against him.

Neither one of them spoke. They simply stood there, under the soft yellow light outside the motel room, each of them coming to terms with this new awareness between them. And the question foremost on both their minds, the question that hung like a dark heavy cloud over them: What were they going to do now?

He'd already tried cold showers, working longer hours and staying away from her. That hadn't worked. She'd still been with him every second of every day.

Perhaps the only way to appease the beast was to feed it, to let it feast until its hunger was satiated.

He wound his fingers into the back of her hair and tugged her head back. She looked up at him, her eyes wide, her lips pink and softly parted. He felt the pounding of his heart and the tightening of every muscle in his body.

There was nothing gentle about his kiss. He crushed his lips against hers and thrust his tongue deeply inside her. He'd expected her to resist his invasion, part of him had *wanted* her to resist. But she didn't. She met him equally, completely, once again surprising him and throwing his equilibrium off balance.

Her lips never left his as she reached behind her and slipped the key into the doorknob. The door to the room opened and they backed inside. She started to reach for the light, but he stopped her, then kicked the door shut and pressed her up against the wall. She clung to him, wrapping her arms around his neck as he cupped her bottom in his hands and lifted her off the floor.

She tasted of lime and salt. And desire. Her slender body molded to his and he knew she'd been made for him. Only for him. He'd spent the past week in denial. Denying that he wanted her, that he needed to feel her body under his and her hands on his skin. What a fool he'd been, to waste what little precious time they had on his damn foolish pride.

He pulled his mouth from hers and sucked in a breath, forcing himself to slow down, when what he really wanted to do was take her right here, to thrust himself deeply into the tight, warm glove of her body and release the unrelenting tension that had been building in him all week.

"Have you any idea what you do to me?" he said raggedly.

She rubbed back and forth against the hard ridge pressing against the juncture of her legs in a slow, sensual movement. "I have a pretty good idea."

He groaned, then took hold of her hips to still her. "You are a wicked woman, Katrina Natalya Delaney."

A wicked woman? Katrina nearly laughed at the thought. No one had ever said *that* to her before. But then, no one had ever done any of this to her before. Made her feel as if she were coming apart, breaking into thousands of tiny white-hot sparks of pleasure.

She needed to move against him, but his hands restrained her. Determined, she started a slow assault on his neck with her mouth. "That's the first time you've said my name without a sneer," she said softly.

His hands tightened on her firm flesh as her warm moist tongue swept over the base of his ear. "Katrina Natalya Delaney," he murmured. "It's a beautiful name."

"Thank you." She nibbled on his earlobe.

He moaned. "Katrina," he said, his voice ragged now, "wrap your beautiful legs around me."

The soft whisper of silk sliding against denim mingled with their breathing as she did what he asked. He kissed her again, pressing her tightly against the wall as he slid up her dress. Her hands roamed over his shoulders then raked up his neck and over his scalp as she struggled to be even closer to him.

She gasped softly as he suddenly moved away from the wall and carried her to the bed. They tumbled down on the soft mattress together and he rolled her underneath him.

Light spilled through the thin inner drapes of the window. He straddled her and sat, raising his body over hers. She shivered at the fierce expression on his face as he gazed down at her.

"You're mine," he whispered tightly. Taking her hands in his, he intertwined their fingers, then raised her arms over her head. "For this moment, you belong to me."

It was a primitive, uncivilized proclamation. A masculine, arrogant display of machismo. And still, his words thrilled her. She *wanted* to belong to him. Completely.

His gentle restraint excited her and she lay under him, her body pulsing with pleasure. She met his gaze and smiled softly. "Yes," she whispered, "and you to me."

His eyes darkened and then his lips sought hers with an urgency that sent her heart racing. He kissed her eyes, her cheek, her jaw, then moved lower, nipping at her bare shoulder, then lower still, dragging his lips over the swell of her breasts as he explored and tasted.

She strained against him, surging upward, wanting her arms free, and yet she was more fully aroused because he still held her pinned to the mattress. His mouth moved lower, but her dress inhibited him from doing what she wanted. She felt his hot breath as his lips moved over the thin cotton, his teeth lightly nibbling over the sensitive flesh.

"Logan," she pleaded, squirming from the unbearable tension building in her. When he laughed softly and ignored her, obviously content with his slow exploration, she cursed him. He only laughed again.

Using his teeth once again, he tugged the top of her dress down. His hot breath skimmed over her awakened skin and she began to tremble with anticipation. When he drew both the thin silk of her bra and the tip of her breast into his mouth, she cried out and bucked under him.

Revenge, that's what this was, she decided. A cruel torture to pay her back for not telling him the truth. A sweet, delicious torture that she might surely die from. She heard the sound of her own whimper and felt herself surrender to him. He'll have his revenge, she acquiesced, then with a sure feminine confidence, she also knew she'd have hers.

The change was subtle, Logan realized dimly. A sudden shift in the urgency radiating from Kat. She moved against him in a slow, seductive manner that was distracting him from the pleasure he wanted to give her. Her cry of need only a moment ago softened to a whisper of enticement. She tempted him, calling to him with her body and her voice, her eyes.

He raised himself over her, holding her gaze with his as he pulled her up, then released her arms and tugged her dress over her head. Her eyes were heavy with passion as she started to slowly unbutton his shirt. When she reached the last button she slid her hands under his shirt and slipped it off his shoulders. He nearly swore when she lightly raked her fingernails through the hair on his chest and slid her hands to the buckle of his belt. He did swear when she released not only the buckle, but the snap of his jeans, as well.

He caught her hands in his and brought them back to his chest, knowing if she touched him anywhere else he would lose it completely. He wanted a little more time, wanted to stretch every minute they shared to the very limit. He covered her hands with his, amazed by their silky texture.

"Your hands are so soft," he whispered, bringing them to his mouth. "I'm afraid I might hurt them."

She closed her eyes as he kissed each delicate fingertip. "They're insured."

He hesitated for a moment, then ran his tongue over one smooth palm. "Really?"

"A million dollars," she said breathlessly.

He raised both brows and whistled softly, kissing the inside of her wrist. He moved up her arm, pausing at the inside of her elbow, then proceeded to her shoulder. She swayed against him, her hands on his shoulders now and he reached behind her, unhooking the snap of her black silk bra. It fell away, exposing her bare breasts to him and he thought he'd never seen anything more perfect.

With his hand behind her shoulder blades, he bent her backward and stared at her naked beauty. "These must be worth at least two million," he teased lightly. She laughed softly, then moaned when he covered one rosy peak with his lips and pulled her hardened nipple into his mouth. She arched into him, raking her fingers through his hair as he tasted the sweetness of her.

She said his name again, tangling her fingers almost painfully in his hair. He turned his attention to her other breast, loving her, reveling in the fact that she was his, if only for this short time.

Her soft pleas turned urgent and it became unbearable, impossible, not to have her under him. He laid her down on the bed and ran his hands up the soft silk of her black hose until he reached the top, then in one fluid motion removed the hose and her black panties. Unable to take his eyes off her, he stripped off his boots and pants and underclothes. He stood over her, felt her watching him, waiting, and when she reached for him he lowered himself on the bed and covered her body with his.

He entered her, groaning with intense pleasure as he slipped into the hot velvet sheath of her body. He could no longer think, he could only feel. She wrapped her legs around him and surged upward, taking him deeper inside her. He felt her nails press into his shoulders and back and he thought he might go crazy from the need he felt.

She strained and writhed beneath him, tightening around him, drawing him still deeper as she sobbed his name. He felt her body ripple and convulse, then her cry of pleasure. His own control snapped then and with a low, guttural sound that was more animal than human he surged deeply into her, again and again, until he felt his body go up in flames.

Minutes later, or perhaps it was seconds, he rolled to his side, bringing her with him and gathering her close. He needed her close to him, close enough to hear the beating of her heart and feel the whisper of her breath on his neck. The air conditioner began to cool their bodies and when she shivered, he reluctantly withdrew from her and tucked them both under the covers. With a contented sigh, she snuggled against him, her eyes closed, her fingers moving quietly over his chest.

He kissed the top of her silky head, her ear, then her soft cheek. When he tasted the salt of her dried tears, he remembered that he'd made her cry and he felt like a heel all over again.

And still, the anger churned in him. Making love had resolved nothing. All they had done was bought themselves a little time.

Time. Right now it was his greatest friend and his worst enemy. He could accept what little time they had left and make the best of it, or he could distance himself again and deny his feelings.

Neither choice appealed to him. And since he'd already tried the latter and the results had been disastrous, his only alternative was to accept his fate.

Kat felt the subtle tightening in Logan's body and the hesitation in his touch. She felt a heavy ache deep in her chest, knowing that reality had once again crashed in on her tumultuous world.

She rose up on one elbow and reached across Logan to turn on the bedside lamp. Light intruded into the room.

He blinked at her and she pulled the sheet up to cover herself and sat.

"All right, Logan," she said with a sigh, "we're going to talk."

He frowned at her. "We already talked."

She shook her head. "We talked about the past, and we talked about the present. What we didn't talk about was the future."

He looked away from her, his lips pressed tightly together. "What's to talk about? You have a world tour. I have a ranch and a family. We'll make do with the time we have left."

His cold, clipped words cut deeply. "Make do?" she repeated quietly. "Is that what we're doing, you and me, we're *making do?*"

She jerked away from him and was nearly out of the bed when his hand closed around her arm and dragged her back. She struggled, but he simply pulled her closer and pinned her under him. She glared up at him, furious, yet aroused at the same time by the press of his hard body on hers.

"Dammit, Kat," he said sharply, "what do you want from me? You want me to tell you that every time I think about you leaving I feel like someone's pulling barbed wire through my gut? You want me to tell you that I feel half-mad knowing you won't be there in the morning when I'm leaving the house, that you won't be there at night, eating dinner with Anna and me?"

His hands tightened painfully on her arms. "Is that what you want? To know that it's killing me that you won't be beside me in my bed and my life? That I've considered more than once tying you up and forcing you to stay? Will knowing that change one damn thing, will it keep you here?''

She stared at him, too stunned to say a word, but knowing at the same time what he said was true. It might make her feel better to know that he cared she was leaving, but it didn't change anything.

His eyes narrowed as he stared down at her and his face was like stone. Suddenly he rolled away from her and sat on the edge of the bed with his back to her.

''Or maybe you want me to tell you I'll chase to the ends of the earth for you.'' His voice was harsher now, more ragged. ''That I'll wait around while you jump from country to country, giving pleasure to thousands of people while I sit at home waiting for postcards and phone calls.''

He combed his hands through his hair and let out a long shaky breath. ''I've already been there, Kat. I will never, *ever,* do that again.''

Kat closed her eyes against the pain that swam through her. She'd been selfish to think that she was the only one affected by her leaving, but until now, she hadn't been sure of Logan's feelings for her, if what they had went beyond the physical for him. She knew now that he did care for her, deeply, but did he love her? And even if he did, it still wouldn't change anything. She still had to leave.

She wanted to tell him she could give it up, that she'd walk away from her contract and her obligations and everyone who counted on her. For one crazy moment, she actually considered it.

But she knew she couldn't. Everything was set in motion. The bookings, the tickets already sold, the people employed. How could she say, ''Sorry, folks, I've fallen in love and changed my mind?'' And it wasn't just the legal ramifications, though getting out of an ironclad contract would certainly be messy. It was much more than that. Commitment and responsibility were important to her. How could she live with herself, be happy, if she let all those people, including her parents, down?

She desperately wanted to tell him that she loved him. But she knew he'd only throw it back in her face, and she wouldn't blame him for that. He'd been hurt before; Anna had been hurt. He wouldn't risk it again and she couldn't ask him to.

Maybe he'd been right. Maybe, after all, it was best to simply "make do." To take the time they had and not think about tomorrow.

"Logan." She reached out to him and he flinched when she touched his back. "We can't change what's happened, nor would I want to. What we can change, what we do have control over is right now. And right now I *am* here, with you and for you. Please," she whispered, "please be here with me, too."

He didn't move for what seemed like years, though it was only seconds. When he finally turned, she saw the softening around his eyes and the loosening of his shoulders. She breathed a deep sigh of relief, and he slipped back into the bed with her and gathered her into his arms.

His lips brushed her neck and he began to nuzzle her shoulder. "Did I tell you that you smell good?"

"Like a bouquet of daisies," she teased, then gasped as his hand slid over her breast.

"Pink daisies." His mouth traveled down to taste where his hand had explored. "Petal soft, like velvet."

His hands and lips began a slow exploration of her body and she felt like the daisy he'd described, a wildflower in an open meadow, swaying lightly in the wind, under the warm sun. She floated with the sensations he created in her, letting the wonderful touch of his hands take her to a place where only the two of them existed. No yesterday, no tomorrow. Only here, only now.

Fourteen little girls screamed all at the same time in Logan's ears. He winced from the pain of it, then jerked upward on the rope holding the mermaid piñata again. The current blindfolded player, a little blond girl named Melissa, swung the stick wildly and missed. Melissa swung again, striking the mermaid's tail hard enough to rip it, but not break it open. The other little girls screamed in excitement at the close call.

He doubted that bombs exploding had the same decibel level as fourteen little girls at a birthday party.

"It's Anna's turn," Julie cried when Melissa took off the blindfold.

Anna glanced over at Kat, who stood a few feet away setting up the cake and presents at a picnic table. Kat smiled and nodded at Anna, and the child hesitantly took the stick Melissa offered her while Julie tied on the blindfold.

Anna had never had a birthday party with other children. She had resisted the idea when Kat had suggested it, but gentle persuasion on Kat's part had finally won Anna's fears over. Fear that no one would come, fear that the other girls might laugh at her or stare. Exactly the same fears that Logan had.

But they had come. A few neighbor girls that Anna knew from town and a few of Julie's friends. They hadn't laughed or stared, though a few had asked Anna what it was like to ride in a wheelchair and did she have one of those cool motorized chairs that she could drive fast. They played games and sang silly songs and ate hot dogs and potato chips. What all little girls did at birthday parties.

"Swing, Anna!" Julie yelled and Anna did, missing the piñata when Logan pulled it upward. She swung again as Logan brought it back down, and this time her blow made a direct hit, breaking open the mermaid's tail and scattering candy all over. Logan scooped up several pieces of chewy taffy and chocolate kisses and tossed them into Anna's lap, and soon all the girls were laughing and tossing candy to Anna.

He'd never seen his daughter so happy.

He'd never been so happy.

He'd never been so miserable.

Dammit, anyway.

He felt his smile slowly fade as he looked at Kat. She was busy lighting the candles on the cake she'd made and her smiling face made his chest ache with longing. Another week had passed, another week of pure bliss and sheer hell.

They'd gone back to the ranch the night after they'd stayed in the motel; he'd had chores at the ranch that couldn't be ignored and he needed to keep a close eye on his mare as her time to foal grew nearer. But after the chores were done, Kat had been waiting for him and they'd spent their time alone together in bed or watching an old movie or just reading together on the couch. Pretty much the same way they'd spent the rest of the week *after* Anna had come home, though he'd sneak into Kat's room later, after his daughter was asleep, then leave before morning.

Neither one of them spoke about her leaving. They'd simply enjoyed every minute, in bed and out. He couldn't stop the smile that spread over his face. Especially in bed.

When she dropped the book of matches and bent to pick it up, he nearly groaned at the sight of her long bare legs and rounded bottom under the white shorts she wore. And when she stood and finished lighting the candles, his gaze settled on the swell of her breasts above her pink sleeveless tank top.

Children's birthday party or not, he knew where he'd like to take her right now. To his bedroom.

She glanced over at him and gave him a look that let him know that she was thinking the same thing. Her eyes softened and she smiled at him, her cheeks flushed. The same flush she always had after they made love.

She pulled her gaze from him and called to the girls. "Time for cake!"

And somewhere between singing "Happy Birthday" and opening presents, he admitted to himself for the first time that he'd fallen in love.

Eleven

He was late.

Kat stared at her clock, then moved to the sliding glass door and looked toward Logan's bedroom. It was almost eleven-thirty and he always came to her room by eleven. With only a week left before she had to go back to New York, every hour, every minute, was critical.

What could be keeping him?

Earlier, after he'd settled Anna in bed, Kat had made him a cup of coffee and they'd talked for a few minutes before he'd gone out to the barn to check on Stardust. The mare had been approaching her time to foal and Logan was keeping a close eye on her anyway, especially since it was her first pregnancy. Kat had been hoping that the horse would give birth soon so she could see the foal, but so far there'd been no definite signs that she was ready.

She looked at the clock again, then shimmied out of her nightgown and slipped on a pair of jeans, a T-shirt and her boots. If the mountain wouldn't come to Mohammed…

It was hot and humid outside and just the walk to the

barn left her skin feeling damp and sticky. It never ceased to amaze her how dark it was here, how many stars there were. How many crickets. She smiled at the discordant insect symphony that was more beautiful, more peaceful than any concerto she'd ever heard.

The light was on inside the barn. She heard the sound of a horse snorting, then Logan's voice, low and deep.

He was in Stardust's stall, she realized, but she couldn't see either one of them. She walked to the open stall and looked in.

Stardust lay on the stall floor, with Logan beside her. He'd put a halter on the horse and held her as he spoke softly. "Steady, girl, take it easy, that's it, baby..."

Careful not to startle the mare, Kat moved closer slowly. "What's wrong?"

He glanced up at her, then quickly turned his attention back to the horse. "She's in labor. Sometimes horses get scared when it's their first time."

Stardust's eyes were wide and filled with terror as she lifted her head and looked back at Kat. "Can I help?"

"You could talk to her, hold the halter for me and try to keep her still while I keep an eye on the birth."

Nervous, yet excited at the same time, Kat knelt on the floor beside Logan. "Is she in pain?"

"She's more frightened than anything else. It'll be easier for her if she stays calm, but it shouldn't be much longer now."

Kat saw the fear in Stardust's big eyes. She stroked the animal's sweating neck and crooned softly. The mare snorted and kept looking at her side in confusion. "You'll be fine, sweetheart. That's a love, it's all right..."

Stardust tossed her head and grunted deeply.

"Front feet are out," Logan said finally from the other end of the horse.

Kat continued to soothe the distraught mare while Logan kept a close eye on the delivery.

"Here's the nose and head," Logan said excitedly.

"You're having a baby, sweetheart," Kat murmured, "a beautiful, wonderful baby."

As if understanding Kat's soft words, Stardust laid her head down and let nature take its course without fighting it.

"All the way now, sweetheart, one more push, that's a girl," Logan encouraged.

Kat held her breath. Her heart pounded furiously against her ribs.

"It's a filly!" Logan looked at Kat and they both grinned.

Kat ran her fingers over the mare's nose while Logan worked over the foal. "You have a daughter, Stardust. Do you know how lucky you are?"

"Looks healthy." Logan examined what looked to Kat like a wet, black mass.

The mare snorted, then lunged suddenly and stood. Kat jumped away, still holding on to the halter and talking quietly to the animal. "What do you do now?" she asked Logan.

"Not much," he answered. "Just get the placenta out of the way and keep it for the vet to check, swab the umbilical separation with iodine, then rub the worst of the birth mess off the foal and stand back while Mama and baby get to know each other."

"Just like people," Kat said, smiling.

"Yeah." Logan smiled back. "Just like people."

Logan was reaching for one of the towels he'd placed in there earlier when Kat asked, "Can I do it?"

He looked at her with surprise. "Clean the foal?"

She nodded.

He hesitated. "It's messy."

"It's not messy," she said softly, "it's a baby."

She never ceased to amaze him, Logan thought as he handed Kat the towel. Before she'd come here, she'd never even seen the inside of a barn. Now here she was, helping deliver a foal as if it were the most natural thing in the world to her.

The mare was calm now, starting to look back at the baby she'd just delivered and sniff the air. Kat let loose of the halter and moved beside Logan.

"What do I do?" she asked.

"Just get the worst of it off." He gestured to the towel he'd given her. "Too much interference might cause Stardust to reject her baby."

"Stardust would never do that." Kat knelt beside the squirming foal and touched the towel to its wet side. "Your mama loves you, Little Stardustie. Mamas never leave their babies."

She was wrong there, Logan thought with a frown. Mamas did leave their babies. Animal and human. He wasn't sure which category to fit his ex-wife in, but she'd certainly walked out and never looked back.

He watched Kat run her hands gently over the foal. The filly's big eyes were wide open, its wet body glistened darkly. "You're beautiful," Logan heard Kat whisper and knew that when she had a child, she would die before she left it.

"Logan, look," Kat said, rubbing at the foal's head, "she has a little white star on her forehead, just like her mama."

The filly made tiny high-pitched noises as it struggled to stand on its sticklike legs. When it finally succeeded, the foal shook its little head and gave a miniature whinny. Stardust answered, then turned in the stall until she could reach her baby.

Kat stepped back with Logan to watch Stardust lick her filly. The baby whinnied again, then began to search for milk.

"It really is a miracle," Kat whispered.

Logan looked at Kat and saw the tears in her eyes and the mess on her hands and he thought that she'd never looked more beautiful to him. He felt a tightening in his chest and fought back a thick feeling in his throat. He'd seen horses give birth dozens of times, but never once had it affected him as it did right now.

But he'd never shared this before with someone that he loved, someone he wanted to share this with again and again. Someone he wanted to have his own children with.

Would she stay if he asked her? he wondered for a crazy moment. If he begged her? He would beg, if it would keep her here. More than life itself, he wanted this woman. Would she give up everything she'd worked for her entire life for him, and for Anna? Would she stay and have his babies and never leave?

His heart hammered against his chest at the thought. It *was* crazy. But so was he. Crazy knowing that she was leaving, crazy that he'd never see her again. That he'd never see her smile or be able to pull her close to him in the middle of the night.

He would ask her. Not now, he'd know when the time was right. Somehow he'd find the right words and the courage and he'd ask.

Kat wrapped her hands in the dirty towel she held then leaned back against Logan. He rested his chin on the top of her head and they watched the foal suckle. After a few quiet minutes, Logan took Kat into the tack room and tossed the towel she'd used into a bin. He held up her dirty hands and looked at them, then put them in the sink and turned on the water.

"Million dollar hands," he said, chuckling as he poured powdered soap into her upturned palms. "I'll bet your insurance company would have a heart attack if they could see you right now."

Laughing softly, she scrubbed her hands, then used a soft brush on her nails. When they were pink and squeaky-clean he handed her a towel, then washed his own hands.

"You know, I came out here with a purpose," Kat said from behind him.

He glanced over his shoulder and saw that she'd closed the tack room door. "Oh? And what was that?"

"To find you." She moved toward him, her eyes darkening to a deep smoky green.

He dried his hands and tossed the towel away. "Well, you found me. Now what?"

"I thought I might do some laundry."

He raised one eyebrow. "Laundry?"

"I thought I'd start with your shirt. It's dirty."

One corner of his mouth twitched upward. "You want me to take it off?"

She smiled and reached for his top button. "Don't bother yourself. I'll do it."

With agonizing slowness, she undid each button, then slipped her hands inside.

"Maybe you'd like to wash my pants, too," he said hoarsely, loving the feel of her smooth warm fingers on his skin. His pulse began to race when she pressed her lips to his chest.

"Hmm, maybe."

Her hands moved over him with velvet softness, while her lips and tongue began to taste his skin and make lazy circles over the tiny nubs of his nipples. He sucked in a sharp breath, then another when her hands moved over his belt, then lower, stroking the hardness she'd already aroused in him.

Like a wild brushfire, flames of desire swept through him. He caught her chin in his palm and lifted her mouth roughly to his, kissing her deeply as he backed her toward the tack room bench. Without breaking the kiss, he reached for a clean towel with one hand while he swept away the brushes and assorted tools lying on the bench, then laid the towel flat on the bench.

In one fluid movement, he unsnapped her jeans and tugged them down. The realization she wore no underwear nearly drove him mad. She gasped as he hoisted her onto the bench. He'd never felt such an urgency with her before, a need to join with her and make her his. He pushed up her T-shirt and the sight of her full, naked breasts made his body throb with need. His mouth closed over the peak of one breast, and with his tongue he circled the rosy pink nipple until it hardened like a pearl. With a soft moan, her head fell back and she closed her eyes. He cupped both swollen breasts in his hands, kneading the feminine flesh as he drew her into his mouth, watching with pleasure as they transformed into tight hard buds under his attention.

When he could stand no more, he spread her legs and moved between them, unsnapping, then pushing his own jeans down. He entered her with a savage thrust and she groaned at the impact of their bodies. Her arms circled his shoulders tightly and she clung to him, her own desire rising as fast and furiously as his. He felt her tighten around him and take him into her deeper. She buried her face in his neck, then gave a shuddering cry as she surged upward. He caught her hips and ground himself against her, then groaned deeply as the coiled tension inside him exploded.

It was a long time before either one of them moved, even longer before they could speak. She lay against him like a rag doll and he dressed her gently, kissing her temple and cheek.

"You'll have to carry me," she whispered when he stood her up.

To her surprise, he did.

"Attention, everyone, attention." Trudy Goodhouse stood center stage of the Harmony High School auditorium and spoke into the microphone. The hall was packed to standing room only, and over the fracas of the crowd, no one heard the music teacher's stern request. Or no one paid attention.

"I said," Trudy repeated sharply and moved closer to the microphone, "*attention!*"

The high-pitched screech reverberated through the auditorium, evoking a chorus of groans and complaints from the crowd. The painful command seemed to work, however, and the hall quieted.

Trudy pushed her glasses up her nose, smoothed the front of her best black satin dress, then smiled with approval at the audience's compliance.

"Welcome, everyone, to the annual Harmony Schools

Extravaganza. As always, it's an honor for me to organize and present to you a program that will showcase the talented musicians of our wonderful town. From tonight's amazingly diverse performers, we will hear first a toe-tapping selection from Leonard Bernstein's *West Side Story,* played by Joseph Green on the piano, and then…"

Kat stood backstage with Anna and Logan, trying her best to calm both father and daughter as Trudy went over the evening's program, naming each performer and the piece they'd be playing.

Anna looked beautiful. Kat had taken the little girl shopping and she'd picked out a white lace dress and white patent leather shoes. She'd loved the dress when she'd seen it in the store and tried it on, but tonight Anna had complained it was awful and she had nothing to wear so she couldn't possibly play. Kat recognized opening night jitters and had reassured Anna that she looked like an angel.

Logan, on the other hand, looked as handsome as the devil in a Western-cut black blazer, dress pants and boots and, of course, his black Stetson. Kat had never seen him dressed up before and the sight of him made her insides turn soft and her head spin.

It also made her heart ache.

Because at ten-thirty tomorrow morning she was flying out of the Dallas airport and going home.

Kat had already had several long talks with Anna about her leaving. Anna had cried every time and asked her to stay, but Kat had explained that she'd made a promise to the people she worked for and she never broke a promise. Kat then made a promise to Anna that she would write often and call when she could.

But Logan hadn't brought up the subject of her leaving even once since the night at the motel. The only mention of it had been yesterday when she'd asked him for a lift into town to catch an early bus to the airport. He'd told her he'd taken care of everything and when she'd tried to discuss the transportation with him, he'd merely ignored her.

In fact, she thought, he'd almost been indifferent to her

leaving, as if it suddenly didn't matter. If anything, he'd seemed happier this week, as if he hadn't a care in the world.

No. She couldn't believe that. He *did* care. She saw it in his eyes, felt it in his touch. It was more than the physical with them, she *knew* it.

And yet he'd been so calm, so nonchalant when he'd heard her check on her plane reservations today. He hadn't said a word, and when she'd spent the afternoon packing, before getting ready for the concert tonight, she'd heard him whistling in the other room.

Had he grown tired of her? Was he actually anxious for her to leave now? The mere thought was like a knife ripping her in two.

But she didn't want to think about it tonight. The fact was, she didn't want to ever think about it. Because if she did, she knew she'd fall apart. Somehow, someway, she would deal with losing the only man she'd ever loved, the only man she ever would love, and the most precious child in the world.

"Kat, I can't do it." Anna suddenly grabbed Kat's hand, pulling her out of her thoughts about Logan. "Tell her to stop, not to say my name."

Kat looked down at the frightened child and forced all thoughts of leaving from her mind. Tonight was Anna's and Kat refused to let anything take away from this special moment. She also knew that a first performance was always the most terrifying, and the only way to overcome that fear was simply to do it.

"Anna, sweetheart," Kat said, kneeling beside Anna, "you *can* do it. You've played this piece beautifully all week."

"No!" Anna's tiny fingers squeezed Kat's hand. "I can't. I forget. I feel sick, I—"

"And on the violin, in her first solo performance," Trudy said from onstage, "we have Anna Kincaid, a remarkable young lady who will be playing a number by Brahms in D minor."

Anna's face paled and she looked at her father for rescue. "Daddy, please don't make me do it," she cried.

More than anything, Logan wanted to take his daughter out of here, away from all these people, away from what was frightening her. All her life he'd made everything safe for her, protected her. But Kat had made him realize that too much protection would only smother, that if he ever wanted Anna to trust herself, to have confidence in herself, she had to take risks. And no matter how difficult it was for him, he had to let her.

"Anna," he said quietly. "I know it's scary, but I also know you can do this."

"I can't," Anna whined. "I'm not good enough."

"You're wonderful," Logan said softly. "You've worked hard to be here tonight, and you made a promise to Miss Goodhouse. You don't want to break that promise, do you?"

Anna bit her lip and lowered her eyes. "I'm scared," she whispered.

"It's okay to be scared." He took her small hand in his. "I get scared sometimes, too."

Anna looked up. "You do?"

"Sure I do. When I'm afraid, I get a funny little feeling in my stomach and my heart goes real fast."

"Me, too!" Anna sat straighter. "And my hands get wet, too."

The first performer began to play. Trudy hurried over and took hold of Anna's wheelchair.

"Time to get you ready," Trudy chirped.

Logan kissed his daughter's cheek. "Knock 'em dead, sweetheart."

Anna's face was pale. "Will you be here? Where I can see you?"

"In the first row," he said. "I wouldn't miss my girl play her violin for anything."

She looked anxiously at Kat. "And you'll be here, too?"

"Right next to your daddy," Kat reassured her, then gave her a hug. "You'll be wonderful."

Anna drew in a deep breath, then looked at Trudy and smiled weakly.

Logan struggled to sit through a Bach cello sonata, then Gershwin's "Rhapsody in Blue" before Anna wheeled herself out. She sat there for a long minute and looked out at the audience, her eyes wide and her back rigid. For one moment Logan thought she might bolt.

But she didn't.

She glanced first at him, then Kat, then she smiled slowly and raised her violin.

He'd heard her play before. Three years ago when he'd first realized she had a remarkable talent, then at the festival. But now, watching her play a piece she'd rehearsed with Kat, and seeing the intensity in her eyes as she performed, he knew he'd been wrong to try to stop her. Kat had tried to tell him, but he'd been wrapped up in his own need to keep his daughter in a cocoon.

He watched his little girl, the child he loved more than life itself, with her pink cheeks and white lace dress and he thought his chest might burst with pride.

When she finished, the room burst into a thunderous applause. He saw the surprise in Anna's eyes as she stared out at the applauding people, then the pleasure. Kat handed him the red roses they'd brought for Anna. When he stood and walked onto the stage to give them to her, the audience went wild again. Logan looked at Kat and she smiled softly at him with tears in her eyes.

And as he looked at the woman who'd brought such a change to his and his daughter's life in these past few weeks, he knew that tonight was the night. His last chance to make her change her mind and stay. He'd rehearsed his speech as diligently as Anna had rehearsed her music.

I love you, Kat Delaney. I need you. Anna needs you. Stay with us. Marry me and love me and have my babies...

He had the craziest urge to step up to the microphone and say those words in front of the whole damn room. She loved him. He knew she did, even though she'd never said the words. And she loved Anna. Wouldn't that mean more to her than anything else? Surely there would be another violinist who could take her place in the tour she'd planned. There had to be someone who could fill in.

He didn't expect her to give it up completely, of course. She could teach and play locally, maybe an occasional benefit or concert, before they had children. The thought of her having his baby brought a smile to his face. Still grinning, he made his way back to his seat.

"And now," Trudy Goodhouse said, stepping up to the microphone, "for those of you who might not know, we have one of the most gifted, most brilliant violinists in the world of classical music right here with us tonight and if we give her a little encouragement, perhaps she'll honor us with her remarkable talent."

The applause began. Logan looked at Kat and saw her freeze, then shake her head stiffly at Trudy, who merely grinned and encouraged the audience to clap louder. He saw the panic in her eyes as she glanced at him.

He smiled slowly at her, then stood and began to clap, too. Surprise replaced the panic in her eyes. He offered her his hand. She hesitated, then smiled slowly and placed her palm in his.

He squeezed her hand as she stood, then released her and watched her walk onto the stage to confer for a moment with Trudy, who just happened to have not only a violin for Kat, but one for herself, also, plus three students waiting to play accompaniment.

He smiled to himself and settled back in his seat. He'd let Trudy and all these strangers have Katrina Natalya Delaney for a little while. But then she was his. All his.

She glanced at him one last time before she raised her violin.

And then she began to play.

The piece had a gypsy quality to it, an intense haunting melody that mesmerized him. He'd had no idea it was possible to evoke that kind of sound from any instrument.

Her fingers danced over the strings, her bow flashed and

the music she played drew the listener to her, took them to a place beyond the physical.

He forgot to breathe.

He saw the intensity on Kat's face, felt the passion shimmer from her, and he felt drawn to her as he never had before. It felt as if she were touching him deeper than any human being ever had, as if she had moved inside the very heart of him and had breathed life where it had never been before.

And he realized in that instant of awareness that everyone in the room felt the same way. That anyone who ever heard her play would experience a melding of mind and body and soul.

He understood now what he couldn't have possibly understood until this moment, and with that understanding came the profound sense of loss.

He knew that he could never ask her to stay. He hadn't the right. Anna had told him that she would quit playing for him, that she would give it up if that was what he wanted. He'd told her no.

No matter how much he loved Kat, or how much he needed her, he couldn't ask her to give up playing, either. It had all been a dream. A fantasy. She would never truly be his, not the way he needed her.

He'd asked himself once if he was glad she'd come into his life and there was only one answer. Yes. His world and Anna's was better because of it.

Letting her go would be the hardest thing he'd ever done in his life and it was going to hurt like hell.

The audience went wild when she finished. She bowed demurely, then acknowledged her accompaniment with a graceful sweep of her arm. Trudy and her students flushed with pride and bowed, as well.

It was always this way for her, Kat thought as she bowed one last time to the audience. The same wild rush of adrenaline, the thrill of knowing that people enjoyed the music she played. It had been that way for her since her first recital at her music teacher's home in New York.

And yet, tonight, something *was* different.

She'd felt the music, she knew she'd played well, but somehow, tonight was not the same as it had always been. There was an emptiness inside her, a feeling that she'd forgotten something, left something out.

She looked at Anna and Logan, saw them watching her, smiling, and the emptiness inside her increased.

Dear Lord, how was she ever going to leave them?

If only he'd talk to her, maybe there was a chance, some way they could work things out. If only he'd wait for her...

She felt the moisture burn her eyes and the room began to blur around her. There'd be no compromise with Logan, he'd made that clear. No concessions, no negotiations. He wouldn't wait for her, and though she wanted to ask him, she wanted to *beg* him, she knew it would do no good.

Later, she wouldn't even remember how she managed to hold the smile on her face and walk off the stage, or that she'd spoken with several people who'd complimented her and even signed a few autographs for her well-wishers.

What she would remember, what she would never forget when she finally made her way back to Logan, was the look of goodbye in his eyes.

Twelve

Logan sat on the hard ground, dust swirling around him, and tried to decide what hurt more, his butt, or his pride.

The horse that had just thrown him stood nearby, calmly munching on a stump of grass, while the steer he'd been chasing bawled insults from the ravine it had run into.

His pride, he decided, clenching his jaw as he readjusted his hat. With a curse, he stood slowly and brushed the dirt off his pants.

He definitely was not having a good day.

Limping to the edge of the ravine, Logan stared at the steep incline, then looked back at his horse.

"Okay, so maybe it was a stupid idea," he said to the animal.

The horse pricked his ears, then threw his head up and down.

Logan glared at the animal. "No need to be so damn agreeable," he muttered.

But the fact was, it *had* been a stupid idea. By refusing

to charge down the incline, the horse had exhibited better judgment than its rider.

He was just lucky he hadn't broke his damn fool neck, not to mention risking injury or death to the horse.

He'd been pushing himself like this for three weeks. Riding harder, bulldozing his way through each day in a kamikaze attempt to drive all thoughts of a green-eyed, slender-curved brunette out of his mind.

It hadn't worked, of course, and the black, empty hole in his gut only got bigger as each day passed.

She'd sent several postcards from New York, addressing them to both Anna and Logan Kincaid. He pulled the latest one from his back pocket, knowing it was silly he carried it with him. The picture was the Statue of Liberty, her note short and superficial. She'd drawn a happy face and written, *Love, Kat.*

JoAnn had sent postcards in the beginning, too. But she'd never drawn a happy face, and he'd never put one in his back pocket and carried it around with him.

With a heavy sigh, he shoved the postcard back into his pocket and sat on the edge of the ravine, letting the hot sun beat down on his back. Driving himself to exhaustion hadn't worked. Maybe he could sweat the frustration and anger out of him. Frustration that the woman he loved would never be his, and anger that there was nothing he could do about it.

He hadn't even kissed her goodbye at the airport. Their eyes had met for one brief moment when the loudspeaker announced her flight had begun to board. He'd seen the sadness there, the moisture in her gray-green eyes, and it had taken a will of iron not to pull her into his arms. But he hadn't. Because if he had, if he'd even touched her, he'd known that nothing on this earth could have stopped him from dragging her back to the ranch with him and Anna.

So he watched her kiss Anna goodbye and walk away. And he kept watching until her plane had taken off, then disappeared completely.

Anna had cried and he'd comforted her, and late that

night, after he'd settled his daughter in bed after another round of tears, Logan had let a bottle of whiskey comfort him. Getting drunk hadn't solved anything, but it had cut the edge off the pain in his chest for a few hours, so he decided it was worth it, despite the miserable headache he'd woken up with the next morning.

And the first thing he'd done, after taking a handful of aspirins, was call Mrs. Lacey and fire her, then enroll his daughter in Harmony Elementary School's fifth grade class starting in two weeks.

Trudy Goodhouse had been thrilled, of course, and had immediately pestered Logan into signing Anna up for band practice. She'd also mentioned a music conservatory in Dallas, but Logan had quickly ended that discussion. He knew that he could no longer ignore Anna's exceptional musical talent, nor did he want to. He watched his daughter bloom these past two months. She not only looked healthier, but she was also more confident and had friends now. No amount of money could have ever brought those changes. Only Kat, with her bright-eyed enthusiasm and quiet determination, had made both Anna and his life better.

He sighed and tossed a handful of pebbles down the ravine. But there were too many changes right now to send Anna away to study. Perhaps next year. This year she'd have a new school, new friends and the position of first violinist in the Harmony Elementary school band.

Anna had written Kat the next day and told her the exciting news. She'd written back and told her how proud she was of her, and how much she missed her.

She'd said nothing about him.

He knew the opening performance on her world tour was at Carnegie Hall one week from today. The day after she flew to London, then Paris, then Rome. Thanks to his new subscription to *Classical Weekly*, he knew he'd be able to follow every performance in every country and city for the next two years.

Three years ago, when the phone call had come after

JoAnn's accident, he hadn't even known what state she was in, let alone what city.

She'd been his wife and the mother of his child, and still, the news of her death had brought only a strange sadness. For JoAnn, of course, because she was so damn young. For Anna, because any opportunity to know her mother was gone forever.

Kat had left only three weeks ago, and already, every time the phone rang, he felt his insides twist and his hand began to shake.

He couldn't live like that. He *couldn't*.

He couldn't live like this.

What the hell was he going to do?

"Katrina, lift your right arm a little higher, dear, or I'm afraid I'm going to stick you with a pin."

"Too late." Kat shifted the sheet music she studied from one hand to the other while her mother knelt on the plush carpeting of the living-room floor and fussed over the last-minute alterations of the gown she'd designed for her daughter's opening performance in exactly six days. It was an exquisite black velvet gown, long and strapless with a slit up the side and a bodice that shimmered from an intricate weaving of tiny gold beads.

"You're fidgeting," Larisa scolded, then frowned as she pinched the waist of the dress. "What is this? You've lost more weight."

"Too busy to eat." Kat pretended great interest in the music in her hands. She didn't want to get started on another discussion about her health or the fact that she'd lost a couple of pounds.

"You've been pushing yourself awfully hard since you got back from Texas," her mother said quietly.

"I'm fine, Mom, really," Kat lied. She hadn't told her mother about Logan. She hadn't told anyone. Not even Oliver. What was the point? There was nothing anyone could say to her, nothing anyone could do. Sympathy would only make her feel worse, if that were possible.

"Speaking of busy," Max said from the sofa where he'd spread out a page-by-page itinerary of every performance for the next three months, "tomorrow we have a ten o'clock meeting with the production manager for the 'Today' show, an eleven-thirty appointment to do a ten-minute interview on satellite for a news program in Austria, then lunch with Sydney, one o'clock at Tavern on The Green."

Kat groaned silently. The appointments were bad enough, but Sydney, of all people. The gossip columnist had called nearly every day for the past three weeks for an interview, but Kat had managed to put her off. She knew that the woman didn't want to talk about music or the tour; she wanted the inside scoop on Logan Kincaid, Texas rancher.

But the only inside scoop was that there *was* no scoop. Not anymore. Kat sucked in a sharp breath at the ache that swelled inside her chest.

Her mother looked up. "Did I hurt you, dear?"

Kat shook her head. Her mother watched her for a moment, her eyes troubled, then sighed and turned her attention back to the dress.

Suddenly she was so tired all she wanted to do was lie down, right here, right now, pins and all, and just go to sleep.

She gave in to the feeling and closed her eyes, but it was Logan and the memory of their last night together that invaded her mind. He'd come to her bed and held her for a long time, cradled her in his arms with a tenderness that had made her cry. He'd kissed her tears, then made love to her slowly, so slowly she thought she might go mad with the passion he aroused in her.

And the love. She'd known that she loved him before that night, but even she hadn't realized how deeply, how completely. Without him, she felt empty and cold.

Kat jumped at the sound of a staccato rap on the front door, forcing at least three straight pins into her waist. Larisa jumped, too, catching the tip of her finger on a sharp point. Oliver strode in looking exceptionally handsome in a pair of jeans, the cowboy boots Kat had sent him from Texas, a black T-shirt and a gray blazer. He carried a brown paper grocery bag in one hand and a bottle of champagne in the other.

"Larisa, Max, you're going to love my magic act," Oliver said brightly as he set his bag on the dining-room table.

"Are you going to disappear?" Larisa asked and sucked at her wounded finger.

Max ignored the commotion and kept sorting through his papers.

Oliver bent to kiss Larisa's cheek. "Katrina, your mother's intelligence and wit are exceeded only by her beauty."

"I am not giving you my new designer's phone number," Larisa said flatly and stood to inspect the adjustments she'd just made on the gown.

"Already have it," he said with a wink. "But thanks for the thought."

Larisa frowned, but Kat saw the smile in her mother's green eyes and couldn't help but smile herself. Oliver had been her one saving grace since she'd come home. Without his silly antics and ridiculous flirting, she would have gone crazy more than once.

"And what feat of magic is Oliver going to perform, you ask?" Oliver stuck his hands into his pocket and pulled out tickets. "Ta-dah!"

Larisa looked closely, then gasped. "You have tickets for *Osborne's Moon?* With George Parkman? Nobody can get those tickets. It's been sold out for weeks."

"And backstage passes." He waved the tickets under her nose. "Word has it George is on the outs with his manager, Max. You just might steal him away."

Max's head snapped up. George Parkman was the hottest new talent on Broadway at the moment, and Max never missed an opportunity to snatch up star material.

"Nicolai is waiting for you at the theater." Oliver looked at his watch. "You have twenty minutes to meet him there."

"But I can't," Larisa said breathlessly. "I can't leave Katrina alone. And I couldn't possibly be ready so fast."

Max had already set aside the papers he'd been sorting through and was reaching for his jacket.

"You're beautiful," Oliver said. "And you're not leaving Katrina alone. I'm making her dinner to fatten her up."

"But her dress—"

"You have a whole week and an entire staff to finish her dress if necessary. Now go."

"But—"

Max was waiting at the open front door, looking at his watch.

Oliver herded Larisa toward the front door, grabbing her sweater and purse from the entry closet, then handing the tickets to Max. "Have a good time, kids. Don't get into trouble, now."

He closed the door, then came back into the living room. Still not sure what had just happened, Kat simply stared in amazement.

"Alone, at last." He rubbed his hands together.

"That *was* a magic act," Kat said with admiration. "Now help me out of this dress."

"Well, I was going to cook for you first, then take your clothes off, but I suppose this works, too."

Laughing, Kat sucked in her breath while he unzipped her dress.

"I'll pour us some champagne while you slip into something more comfortable, my dear." He wiggled his eyebrows.

Kat shook her head and headed for her bedroom. "You are outrageous, Oliver Grant. Someday you're going to get yourself into trouble."

"I'm afraid I already have," she heard him say as she slipped out of the dress and pulled on a pair of old sweats and a tank top.

He was standing in the dining room when she came back, pouring two glasses of champagne. He frowned at her apparel. "You didn't have to take me so literally about being comfortable. I was thinking silk and lace."

Kat rolled her eyes. "Enough, already. Tell me what we're celebrating."

He smiled. "I'm getting married."

"Married?" She wrinkled her brow. "You?"

His eyes softened as he looked at her. He reached into his pocket, pulled out a black velvet ring case and flipped it open as he handed it to her. "Well, at least I hope I am. I haven't asked her yet."

Kat went very still. She stared at the sparkling diamond ring, then slowly lifted her eyes. "Ollie, I...I—"

It was Oliver's turn to roll his eyes. "Not you, silly. It's Sharon Westphal."

"The flutist?"

He was grinning like a man in love. "Blonde, baby blue eyes, the most wonderful girl in the world. Well, after you, of course."

She stared at him. "*You*, Oliver Grant, confirmed bachelor and playboy, are asking Sharon Westphal to marry you?"

"Don't look so surprised. You're responsible, you know. If you hadn't kept pushing, I never would have even asked her out. I was terrified of her. So sweet and innocent and much too good for me."

"True," Kat agreed. She laughed when Oliver frowned at her, then hugged him. "I still can't believe it, Ollie. You, married."

"Well, I would have asked you first, of course, but since you're already in love with someone else, I knew you'd just turn me down anyway."

She went very still at his words, then pulled away. "*What* did you just say?"

"I said I would have asked you first, but—"

"*Oliver...*"

He lifted one eyebrow and sighed. "Katrina, my darling, it's as plain as the nose on your pretty little face. You're madly in love and miserable. Don't you think it's time you told me about it?''

Why did she think she could hide anything from Oliver? He knew everything about her, and she about him, though he'd certainly thrown her with the news of getting married. If she hadn't been so self-absorbed, she would have realized something was going on with her friend.

She sighed and sank onto a dining-room chair. ''There's nothing to tell, not anymore,'' she said softly. ''It's over.''

''It's hardly over.'' Oliver turned a chair around and straddled it. ''You still love him, and there's no doubt he loves you. He'd be a fool if he didn't.''

She smiled at her friend's loyalty. ''It's complicated. He doesn't want a career wife, especially a well-known violinist who has to travel a lot. His first wife put him and his daughter through hell. He won't go through it again, not for me, not for anyone.''

''Have you thought of canceling the tour?''

Startled, she looked at him. ''Don't be ridiculous. I have a contract, a commitment and responsibility.''

''Ah, the age-old dilemma,'' Oliver lamented. ''Duty versus love.''

That's what her career had become, Kat realized sadly. A duty. ''Music has always been everything to me, the soul of my existence. Now, without Logan and Anna, even my music feels empty and flat. *I* feel empty and flat.'' She sighed heavily. ''Everyone's counting on me, Ollie. Max, my parents, all the other musicians. I can't just walk away.''

''There are ways,'' Oliver suggested. ''Replacements, change of programs. People get sick all the time. Every contract has to allow for medical problems.''

''I'm not sick.'' She folded her arms on the table and rested her chin on her hands. ''I just feel like it.''

''You give up too easily, Katrina,'' Oliver said softly. ''I thought you had more backbone than that.''

''Well, I don't,'' she muttered. ''I'm too tired. And even if I did, I'm still Katrina Natalya Delaney. If he can't accept who I am, and what comes with me, what chance would we have, anyway?"

"There's always a chance, my love. Even the tallest man riding on the tallest horse has to fall sometime. When he does, it'll knock a little sense into him."

She almost laughed at the appropriate image for Logan. She'd love to see it in person.

"I don't want to talk about Logan or me anymore. I'm going to be fine," she said, though she knew it wasn't true. "I've been a terrible friend and I apologize for not being more aware of what's going on with you. Tell me about you and Sharon. What in the world does a sweet girl like her see in a rogue like you?"

Oliver grinned and stretched out his long legs. "It was these cowboy boots you sent me. She went wild for me when I wore them on our second date. There really is something to that Western mystique, after all."

Kat laughed softly and laid her head on her arms. Oliver kissed her cheek. "We'll talk more later. You sleep and I'm going to cook you a meal that would make the angels cry."

They already were crying, Kat thought dimly as she closed her eyes and drifted off. And there was nothing she could do to change that.

The hall was alive with concertgoers, women in black evening gowns and diamonds, men in tuxedos and bow ties. Like a sparkling river, everyone moved toward their seats. Excitement floated on the evening air, mingling with the scent of expensive perfumes and huge displays of fresh flowers placed throughout the lobby. Conversations were hushed, almost reverent as they eagerly anticipated Katrina Natalya Delaney's opening performance of her world tour.

But no one anticipated seeing Katrina more eagerly than the six-foot-four tuxedo-clad man wearing a black Stetson and cowboy boots.

Anna sat in her wheelchair beside her father, her eyes huge as she looked around the plush lobby. She'd never traveled before and the excitement of the trip, and the fact that she was going to see Kat perform here in this fancy place, had the child nearly jumping out of her chair. She had on the same dress she'd worn for her own performance at the Harmony Schools Extravaganza, and she carried a bouquet of daisies.

Pink daisies.

He'd bought them impulsively from a vendor inside the hotel where they were staying, with impulsive being the key word to describe this whole trip. He still wasn't sure how it had happened. All he knew was that one minute he was holding one of Kat's postcards, and the next minute he'd made plane and hotel reservations and was packing his and Anna's bags.

And now they were here. In New York City. He'd been here before and hadn't especially liked it, but this time was different. This time the town seemed more alive to him, more vibrant. Was it because he knew Kat lived here, or because he no longer looked at life with the same cynicism he had before? Both, he decided.

"Logan Kincaid?"

Logan turned and watched a good-looking blond man in a tuxedo making his way toward him. Logan recognized Oliver Grant from his picture in tonight's program. It didn't seem to matter that Kat had told him she and Oliver were only friends, Logan still felt a flash of jealousy, knowing that this man could see Kat anytime he wanted, that he and Kat would be traveling together for the next two years.

What the hell am I doing here? Logan asked himself as Oliver approached. *It won't change a thing, it won't make me feel any better.*

You'll get to see her one more time. Then put her out of your mind and get on with your life.

"Oliver Grant," the man said, sticking out his hand. "The performance starts soon, so I only have a minute."

Logan took the offered hand. "I appreciate all your help at this late date. Our plans were rather spur-of-the-moment, and we wanted to surprise Kat—I mean, Katrina. I hadn't realized the tickets were sold out, and I didn't know who else to call."

"No trouble at all. Sold-out tickets are my specialty. Besides," he said with a grin, "I love surprises."

Oliver glanced down at Anna and smiled. "And you must be Anna. You're just as pretty as Katrina told me you were."

Anna blushed at Oliver's compliment, then giggled when he kissed her hand. "Are you Kat's friend?" she asked. "Can we see her after the show?"

"I am, and you can. Just ask your daddy to bring you backstage after the performance and tell them you're with me. Okay?"

Oliver shook Logan's hand again, then left, whistling.

Logan felt the knot in his stomach tighten. He knew she'd be happy to see Anna, but how would she feel about him? In the middle of all this glitz and glamour, was a Texas rancher already just a distant memory for her?

It didn't matter, he told himself. They'd say hello and that would be it. He and Anna would sightsee for the weekend and Kat would be off for Europe. He'd never expected any more than that.

The lights were already dimming when Logan and Anna took their seats. He had no idea how Oliver had managed it, but their places were in the third row, with a special provision for a wheelchair on the end of the aisle.

The room applauded when the conductor came out, then quieted when he turned to present Kat. When she walked out, there was a collective gasp from the audience.

The only word to describe her was *stunning*. Her strapless dress was like a glove of black velvet and gold, the slit up the long skirt revealing a lengthy portion of one sleek leg. She wore her hair up, accentuating her long, slender neck and smooth, bare shoulders. Pearls dangled from her ears as she smiled at the audience then took her place beside the conductor.

"Isn't Kat pretty, Daddy?" Anna whispered.

He simply nodded because he hadn't the voice to speak.

He watched her play, but the music, as magical as it was, became background noise. There was only Kat, the woman he loved, the woman he needed more than his next breath.

He'd told himself that he'd see her this one last time and walk away. That he'd get over her, get on with his life just fine without her.

Idiot. That's what he was. A damn stupid fool.

And he knew, at that instant, that no matter what it took, no matter what he had to do or how long he had to wait, she was going to be his. His wife. His love. The mother of his daughter and the mother of his babies.

He nearly laughed out loud at the realization, and when he settled back in his seat he knew that anyone looking at him must think he was some kind of a grinning fool. Which he was. He just didn't give a damn what anyone thought.

It took every ounce of willpower not to stand up and yell, "Stop the music! I love Katrina Natalya Delaney, and she's going to be my wife." But he didn't, of course. He waited, impatiently, through her first piece, through the intermission and the second performance, then through the lengthy and exuberant applause.

Flowers flooded the stage. Smiling, she stepped forward and he noticed how pale she looked, how delicate. He moved toward her, not caring his pink daisies were inadequate next to the elaborate bouquets of red roses. Her smile began to fade as her arms overflowed. He moved closer to her, saw her hesitate, then falter. He called to her and she turned slowly toward him.

Their eyes met, and he watched helplessly as she swayed, then collapsed on the stage.

If they didn't let him see her soon, he was going to tear the place apart.

Logan paced the small waiting room of the hospital, his body coiled tighter than a bale of wire. He looked at his watch, muttered a curse and turned toward the nurse's station.

"Logan," Oliver said calmly from his chair a few feet

away, "they'll call you when they know something. Come play a game of Go Fish with Anna and me, though I warn you, your daughter's a hustler at this game. She's up five licorice sticks and four sticks of strawberry bubble gum."

Logan ran his hands through his hair. He appreciated Oliver entertaining Anna for the past hour. She'd always been frightened of hospitals and doctors, and Logan knew that being here and worrying about Kat was hard on his daughter.

As it was for him.

With a heavy sigh, he sank into a chair and closed his eyes. What the hell was taking so long? He knew her parents were in the examining room with her, but they hadn't come out with any kind of report yet. They hadn't left her side since she'd fainted, and had even ridden in the ambulance with her. By the time Logan had arrived at the hospital with Anna, Kat had already been taken into a room. If Oliver hadn't seen him, Logan knew he'd be stuck in the main waiting room outside with Kat's manager and the press and everyone else who'd come to wait for news.

Logan wasn't sure why Oliver had been so helpful, but he knew he owed the man a big debt.

"Mr. Kincaid?"

He stood abruptly at the sound of a man's deep voice. Kat's parents stood in the doorway, their evening clothes slightly rumpled, but still the model of elegance.

Nicolai put an arm around his wife's shoulders, and she leaned against him. His face was rigid, and Larisa's eyes were red, as if she'd been crying. They both looked exhausted.

Something was wrong. Logan could feel it. And he also felt fear. Heart-stopping, stomach-twisting fear.

"What's wrong?" He moved in front of them.

"Logan," Larisa began, then stopped. "May we call you Logan?"

He nodded at the woman, amazed that even under the most stressful situation, Kat's mother still radiated gentility and refinement. She looked at Anna then, and her face softened. "And this is your daughter we've heard so much about."

He wondered for a moment what Kat had told her mother and father about him, or if she'd told them anything at all about their relationship. If she had, it might explain why Nicolai was looking at him so sternly.

Larisa moved away from her husband and knelt beside Anna. "I'm Katrina's mother. She tells me you play the violin like an angel."

"Is Kat going to be all right?" Anna asked.

Larisa smiled softly. "She's going to be fine, dear. She just fainted, that's all."

Thank God. Logan let loose of the breath he'd been holding. He had to see her now. He had to touch her, kiss her. Pull her into his arms and tell her that he loved her.

He was already turning toward the door when Larisa stood and frowned at Oliver. "Katrina just told me that you're getting married," she said, folding her arms. "Is this true?"

It took a very long heartbeat for the woman's words to sink in, then another heartbeat to understand them.

Getting married...

Katrina and Oliver?

They couldn't be getting married. She'd told him that she and Oliver were only friends. How could all that change in just a few short weeks?

In shock, Logan watched Larisa hug Oliver. Kat belonged to him, not to Oliver! Didn't all these people know that? Pain shot through him, then fear. Fear that he'd truly lost her, that he'd been too stubborn, waited too long.

His pride told him to take Anna and leave quietly, not to make a scene in front of Kat's family.

His heart told him to find the woman he loved and shake some sense into her.

Teeth clenched, eyes narrowed, he brushed past Kat's father and headed for her room.

"Nicolai," Larisa called to her husband when he started to follow the impetuous young man, "leave him be. I believe Mr. Kincaid has something important to say to our daughter.''

Kat was sitting in the hospital bed, tolerating the nurse taking her blood pressure for the third time, when the door flew open. She jumped at the unexpected invasion, as did the nurse beside her.

A very handsome, very angry-looking Texas rancher stood in the doorway, his dark eyes blazing under the brim of his black Stetson, his face as hard as granite.

''Logan!''

''Sir—'' the nurse began, ''you're going to have to—''

''When did you plan on telling me?'' he asked tightly, ignoring the nurse.

Logan? Here? Kat's head began to spin as she watched him move into the room. Why hadn't anyone told her he was here? And why was he wearing a tuxedo? Had he come to her performance? Then she remembered…just before she'd fainted she'd thought that she'd seen him, holding pink daisies as he walked toward the stage. But she thought she'd imagined him.

She knew he'd asked her something. *When did you plan on telling me?* What did he mean? And why was he so angry?

Unless he knew. Her heart began to pound wildly.

''Tell you?'' she repeated, though her voice was barely a whisper.

''Didn't you think I had a right to know?'' He stood beside her bed, his fists clenched at his sides. ''Don't you think a decision like this, a decision that would affect us both for the rest of our lives, is something I should be told?''

''Well, of course, Logan,'' she said nervously. ''And I planned on telling you. But certainly not like this.''

A muscle twitched in his jaw. ''So when? After the fact, I suppose? When it would be too late to do anything about it?''

Her heart stopped. She stared at him, too stunned to even speak. A pain sliced through her like nothing she'd ever felt before. Not even leaving him had hurt this deeply, this sharply. She knew the nurse was watching, but at this point it didn't matter.

Still, she refused to cry. She swallowed through the thickness gathering in the back of her throat and lifted her chin. "I don't know why you came here tonight, Logan, or why you're in New York, but I think you better leave."

His eyes narrowed to dark slits. "I came here for you, *Katrina,*" he said sarcastically. "I came here willing to do whatever I had to do, crawl or beg or both. I was willing to wait for you, two years or ten, whatever it took, whatever your terms were. I'd settle for postcards and phone calls, just as long as I knew that when you did come back, it would be to me, as my wife and the mother of my daughter and the mother of all the rest of my children."

His wife? Mother of his children? Confused and stunned, all Kat could do was stare. Had the man fallen off one horse too many?

He drew in a deep breath and ran his hands through his hair. "I love you, Kat, and I know you love me. I don't know why you're marrying Oliver, but I won't let you. You're going to marry me."

Marry Oliver? What in the world was he talking about? *You're going to marry me.*

His words sank in and the pain that had encased her only a moment ago faded. In its place she felt a profound joy, a happiness that was almost too much to bear. She began to laugh. Bewildered, Logan stared at her. So did the nurse, who had settled back and seemed to be enjoying the show.

"What's so damn funny?" He frowned at her.

In her wildest dreams, Kat never would have thought she'd be laughing hysterically when Logan pronounced his love and proposed. But her emotions were on overload and she found she simply couldn't stop.

"You thought—" she began to hiccup "—that Oliver...and I..."

She was laughing too hard to finish. Logan's frown deepened, but there was also a sudden light in his eyes, an awareness that perhaps he'd made a mistake.

"I heard your mother say you told her that you and Oliver were getting married," he said irritably.

"No, dear," Kat's mother said from the doorway. "I said that Katrina told me that *Oliver* was getting married."

Logan looked more confused than ever. He watched as Kat's parents and Oliver and Anna came into the room, then looked back at Kat. "Well, then what were *you* talking about just now, if it wasn't marrying Oliver?"

Kat hiccuped again, then reached for Logan's hand and pulled him closer. "I—that is, *we're* pregnant."

"Pregnant?" he whispered. "But how, I mean, we were very—" Logan stopped and looked at Kat's parents, then cleared his throat. Her mother was smiling, but her father had a definite scowl on his face.

Kat hardly thought this was the moment to remind Logan about the time in the tack room, after the foal had been born. They'd both been too caught up in each other to think about birth control. Or maybe, just maybe, Kat thought, this was what she'd wanted all along. A baby. Logan's baby.

She hadn't known until tonight, when the doctor came back with his report. She'd thought her exhaustion and food sensitivity were due to stress. Even up on stage, when the smell of the flowers had overcome her, she'd still thought it was nerves. When the doctor had told her she was pregnant, she'd felt like dancing. Her parents' initial reaction was shock, but she knew once they got used to the idea, they were going to be wonderful grandparents.

Actually, they already were grandparents, she thought with a smile as she looked at Anna. Larisa stood beside the little girl, her hand on her shoulder, and it was obvious to Kat that her mother was already feeling protective of the little girl.

Kat waved Anna to come over by the bed, then gave her a hug.

"How would you like to be a big sister?" Kat asked her. Beaming, Anna looked up at her father and nodded. He smiled at his daughter and ruffled the top of her head, then bent and pressed a kiss to Kat's lips.

"Are you sure you're all right?" he asked.

It felt so good to be near him again, to feel his mouth on hers. "I'm wonderful," she said, touching his cheek. "And so is the baby. I'm just a little sensitive to smells right now. All those flowers overpowered me."

Logan straightened, then moved in front of Kat's parents and took off his hat. "I apologize for any embarrassment I've caused you," he said evenly. "But I love your daughter, and if she'll have me, I'd like her to be my wife."

Nicolai studied Logan for a long moment, then offered his hand. "It's about time Katrina was on her own," he said abruptly. "We thought the girl was never going to get married."

"Dad!" Kat choked out, but saw the smile in her father's eyes.

"Welcome to the family, my dear." Larisa stood on her tiptoes and kissed Logan's cheek. "Something tells me that life isn't going to be boring. Come along, Nickie. And Anna, you must come tell me all about life on a ranch. It's so fascinating."

Kat watched as her parents wheeled Anna out of the room, asking her about cows and horses. Oliver, who had been leaning against the back wall, straightened and turned to leave.

"Oliver." Logan walked over to the other man. "I owe you a great deal. If there's anything I can do."

Oliver started to shake his head, then paused and smiled slowly. "Actually there is something."

"Anything."

Oliver looked down at the hat in Logan's hands. "That's a Stetson, isn't it?"

Logan looked at the hat, then handed it to Oliver. "It's yours."

Grinning broadly, Oliver slipped the hat on his head and tipped it forward. "Wait until Sharon sees this," he said, then winked at Kat and left.

Logan started to close the door, then glanced at the nurse who'd been quietly watching the Delaney-Kincaid drama. She smiled dreamily at him, then suddenly realized he was waiting for her to leave. She quickly gathered her chart, then paused at the door, sighed heavily and closed it behind her when she left.

Kat laughed, then gasped as Logan climbed on the bed with her and pulled her into his arms.

"I love you." He brushed his lips against hers.

"And I love you."

"Marry me now," he whispered. "Before you leave."

His kiss, his touch, sent her senses spinning. God, how she'd missed him. "Leave?"

"On your tour." His lips moved to her neck. "We could have a small ceremony here, in New York, with your family."

"Logan, about my tour—"

"It's all right, Kat. I understand that you have to do this. I'm not afraid of it anymore, not as long as I know you're coming home to me and to Anna."

"Logan—"

"Maybe I could join you somewhere in a few days, for a quick honeymoon. You do get a day off occasionally, don't you?"

"Logan—"

His lips moved to her ear. "I'll take whatever you have, a day, a few hours, it doesn't matter."

"Logan!" She sat and took his face in her hands. "I'm not going on my tour."

"You're not?"

She shook her head. "Medical conditions is one of the exclusionary clauses in my contract."

He frowned. "Is being pregnant a medical condition?"

"If I want it to be."

"Do you?"

"Yes," she said softly and smiled. "I most certainly do."

He kissed her again, deeply this time, and long. She

could only imagine what her chart would say if the nurse took her vital signs now. And when he pulled his lips from hers and gathered her close, she felt as if she'd come home, as if here, in Logan's arms, was the only place she was ever meant to be.

"But what's going to happen?" he asked quietly. "What about your bookings, and everyone else involved?"

"They'll have to scramble, find out who's available when to fill in for the different performances, but it can be done. The show does go on, Logan, even without me. And who knows, I might even make a surprise appearance here and there, if I feel like it and my husband and daughter feel like traveling on holidays and school breaks."

"Kat," he said after a long, quiet moment, "I don't want you to ever be sorry, to regret anything that—"

She put her fingers on his lips. "The only thing I could ever regret is if I let the only man I've ever loved, and ever will love, get away from me. How much could my life or my music mean to me, then?" She kissed him lightly and smiled. "I've always wanted to teach, and Anna is going to need a good coach, too. With all that and the baby, there'll be no time for regrets."

"Think you could fit me in there, somewhere?" he teased.

"I think I could definitely fit you in there." She brought his mouth to hers and savored the taste of his lips. "Now, cowboy, let's say we take our daughter and go home."

*　*　*　*　*

IN CELEBRATION OF MOTHER'S DAY, JOIN
SILHOUETTE THIS MAY AS WE BRING YOU

a funny thing

HAPPENED ON THE WAY TO THE

DELIVERY Room

THESE THREE STORIES, CELEBRATING THE
LIGHTER SIDE OF MOTHERHOOD, ARE
WRITTEN BY YOUR FAVORITE AUTHORS:

KASEY MICHAELS
KATHLEEN EAGLE
EMILIE RICHARDS

When three couples make the trip to the delivery
room, they get more than their own bundles of
joy…they get the promise of love!

Available this May,
wherever Silhouette books are sold.

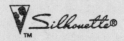
Silhouette®
™

Coming in March from

HOW TO CATCH A PRINCESS

A fun and sexy new trilogy
by LEANNE BANKS

Meet Emily, Maddie and Jenna Jean. As little girls, each dreamed of one day marrying her own Prince Charming.

Sometimes you have to kiss a lot of frogs before you meet the perfect groom. And three childhood friends are about to pucker up!

THE FIVE-MINUTE BRIDE (#1058, March 1997)—
Runaway bride Emily St. Clair hightails herself off into the arms of a rough-and-rugged sheriff.

THE TROUBLEMAKER BRIDE (#1070, May 1997)—
Expectant single mother Maddie Palmer disrupts the life of the tough loner who helps deliver her baby.

THE YOU-CAN'T-MAKE-ME BRIDE (#1082, July 1997)—
Rule follower Jenna Jean Andrews reluctantly learns to have fun with her rule-breaking childhood nemesis.

Don't miss a single one of these wonderful stories!

Beginning next month from

SILHOUETTE® Desire®

The Family McCormick

by
**Elizabeth
Bevarly**

Watch as three siblings separated in childhood
are reunited and find love along the way!

ROXY AND THE RICH MAN (D #1053, February 1997)—
Wealthy businessman Spencer Melbourne finds love with the
sexy female detective he hires to find his long-lost twin.

LUCY AND THE LONER (D #1063, April 1997)—
Independent Lucy Dolan shows her gratitude to the fire
fighter who comes to her rescue—by becoming his slave
for a month.

And coming your way in July 1997—
THE FAMILY McCORMICK continues with the wonderful
story of the oldest McCormick sibling. Don't miss any of
these delightful stories. Only from Silhouette Desire.

National Bestselling Author

MARY LYNN BAXTER

"Ms. Baxter's writing...strikes every chord within the
female spirit."
—Sandra Brown

LONE STAR
Heat

SHE is Juliana Reed, a prominent broadcast journalist whose
television show is about to be syndicated. Until the murder...

HE is Gates O'Brien, a high-ranking member of the
Texas Rangers, determined to forget about his ex-wife. He's
onto something bad....

Juliana and Gates are ex-spouses, unwillingly involved in an
explosive circle of political corruption, blackmail and murder.

In order to survive, they must overcome the pain of the past...and
the very demons that drove them apart.

Available in September 1997 at your favorite retail outlet.

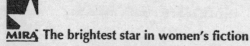

MIRA The brightest star in women's fiction   MMLBLSH

In April 1997
Bestselling Author

DALLAS SCHULZE

takes her Family Circle series to new heights with

TESSA'S CHILD

In April 1997 Dallas Schulze brings readers a
brand-new, longer, out-of-series title featuring the
characters from her popular Family Circle miniseries.

When rancher Keefe Walker found Tessa Wyndham he
knew that she needed a man's protection—she was
pregnant, alone and on the run from a heartless past.
Keefe was also hiding from a dark past...but in one
overwhelming moment he and Tessa forged a family
bond that could never be broken.

Available in April wherever books are sold.